'You must have thought all your Christmases had come at once when Tom Challender, one of the wealthiest men in Western Australia, had a heart attack right at your feet!'

'What?' echoed Jo in astonishment.

'Oh, yes, I like the injured innocence! You do it so well. You don't seriously think you're the first grasping little schemer who has thought she could get her hooks into a lonely old man, do you?'

'I had no idea who your uncle was,' said Jo in a voice shaking with rage. 'I thought he was an old age pensioner, and his name means nothing to me even now.'

'What?' demanded Rob mockingly. 'You've never heard of Tom Challender, the reclusive mining magnate, who discovered one of the richest gold fields in Western Australia?'

'No I have not! But I met a sweet old man who thought the sun shone out of his nephew Bob, and I can tell you this. Tom Challender may know a lot about mining, but he's a hell of a judge of character. Now, if you'll excuse me, I've been insulted enough. I'm leaving!'

Angela Devine was born in Tasmania and took a Ph.D. in Classics. After several years as a university lecturer in New South Wales, she returned to Tasmania to try her hand at writing. With a hospital plot in mind, she pounced on several medical friends for the necessary background. Fortunately her next door neighbour is a surgeon, who has kindly performed many operations into her tape recorder. She is married to an American marine biologist and has four children. Her interests are sailing, archaeology and classical music.

Previous Titles

UNCERTAIN FUTURE
FAMILY MATTERS

CROCK OF GOLD

BY
ANGELA DEVINE

MILLS & BOON LIMITED
ETON HOUSE   18–24 PARADISE ROAD
RICHMOND   SURREY   TW9 1SR

First published in Great Britain 1991
by Mills & Boon Limited

© Angela Devine 1991

Australian copyright 1991
Philippine copyright 1991
This edition 1991

ISBN 0 263 77380 9

Set in 10 on 10½ pt Linotron Baskerville
03-9109-61025
Typeset in Great Britain by Centracet, Cambridge
Made and printed in Great Britain

CHAPTER ONE

'Do YOU mind if I join you, love?'

Jo looked up and saw an old man with a weather-beaten face and blue eyes that twinkled under bushy black eyebrows. She set down her tray, briskly unloaded the food from it, and flashed him a quick smile. Her freckled nose crinkled, her amber eyes lit up and her lips parted, revealing perfect white teeth. Although she was twenty-seven years old, Jo had the exuberance of a schoolgirl. And somehow, whenever she smiled, everybody around her wanted to join in.

'Of course I don't mind!' she said warmly, brushing back a tawny-brown curl from her cheek. 'The tables are filling up pretty fast, aren't they?'

'Too right,' agreed the old man. 'They serve the best counter-lunches in Perth here, that's why. Come on, let me take your tray back for you, lass.'

But as he reached for her tray the old man suddenly gave a low gasp and clutched instead at the side of the table. Concerned, Jo stepped forwards and took his arm. She saw that his face had turned suddenly grey and perspiration was standing out on his brow.

'Are you all right?' she asked.

Tablets. Right pocket,' he gasped.

Reaching into his lightweight jacket, Jo took out a small brown bottle with a plastic lid. She shook a white Anginine tablet into her palm, and handed it to him. Then she poured him a glass of water from a carafe that stood on the table, and watched closely as he slipped the tablet under his tongue. When it had dissolved he reached for a second one. Jo took his wrist and felt for his pulse. As she had expected it was rapid and thready, but his breathing was returning to normal.

5

'Now you sit down and give those a chance to work,' she instructed firmly. 'I'll take the trays back. Would you like a drink while I'm over at the bar?'

'A beer—an alcohol-free one,' he whispered. 'Here, take some money. And buy yourself a drink too while you're there.'

'No, really,' Jo protested. 'I'll get the drinks!'

But the old man was already fumbling with a thread-bare wallet that contained only a worn five-dollar note and a few silver coins.

'Go on,' he insisted, prising out the note with shaking fingers.

Unwilling to upset him further, Jo took the money with a troubled smile, and hurried across to the bar. While she waited among the crowd to be served, she kept her eyes glued on the old fellow and, the minute she had the drinks in her hands, she hurried back to the table. To her relief, he was already beginning to look a little better. Setting the beer down in front of him, she zipped the change into his wallet, and tucked it carefully back into his jacket, which he had hung over the back of his chair.

'Isn't there anyone with you?' she asked with concern.

The old man looked slightly guilty.

'I've given them the slip for the afternoon,' he admitted. 'They fuss over me that much I can't bear it sometimes. Especially my nephew Bob. He's a great bloke, but he makes me feel like a big baby. Still, don't you worry about me, love. I've got a mate picking me up in the car at two o'clock once I've finished me dinner.'

'That's good,' said Jo with relief. 'You know, you really shouldn't be out on your own with heart trouble like that.'

'How did you know it was heart trouble?' rejoined her companion with interest. His alarming greyness was rapidly disappearing, and he now unrolled his napkin from around his knife and fork and prepared to attack the mound of steak and potato and salad in front of him.

'I recognised the tablets,' explained Jo. 'I'm a nurse. My name's Jo Webster, by the way.'

'Pleased to meet you, Jo,' replied the old man. 'My name's Tom. Where are you nursing, love?'

'Nowhere at the moment,' said Jo. 'As a matter of fact, I only arrived in from Sydney a few days ago, but I'm hoping to get a job at the St Jude's Children's Hospital. I've got an interview there this afternoon.'

'Well, the best of luck to you,' said Tom, raising his glass to her. 'I reckon those kids will get well the minute they see your lovely, cheerful face smiling down at them. They'd be bloody fools if they didn't!'

Jo laughed aloud and picked up her orange juice.

'Well, I'll just have to hope for the best,' she smiled. 'Thanks for the drink, Tom.'

The orange juice was freshly squeezed, filled with shreds of fresh fruit and clinking with ice, and the rest of the meal was equally delicious. Charcoal-grilled steak, steaming jacket potato with chives and sour cream and a crisp garden salad. Jo ate hungrily enough, but her thoughts were elsewhere. She desperately wanted the job at St Jude's. Not only because she loved nursing with children, but also because her funds were running out. The air fares to Perth had been very expensive, and she couldn't go on staying with her friend Mary Lou much longer. Not when Mary Lou had two toddlers in a tiny house. . . Jo came back to earth and looked at her watch.

'One forty-five,' she said aloud. 'I must go—I've got a bus to catch. It was nice meeting you, Tom.'

'You too, love,' said the old man, reaching out one frail hand to her. 'You put me in mind of my late wife Bet. She was always full of life too. Well, all the best, Jo.'

Jo smiled. Picking up her bag with all her money and nursing certificates inside, she slung it over her shoulder, and took Tom's hand.

'You will go straight home when you finish here, won't you?' she urged.

'Scout's honour,' agreed Tom with a wink.

Impulsively Jo bent down and kissed his withered cheek.

'Good luck, Tom!' she said. 'Take care.'

Jo was still waiting impatiently at the bus stop ten minutes later when Tom came out the door of the hotel. She waved cheerfully to him, and then suddenly realised that he wasn't wearing his jacket.

'Tom! You've left your jacket inside!' she called.

He made an exasperated gesture and turned back towards the door, and at the precise moment two things happened. The bus squealed to a halt amid a cloud of petrol fumes and Tom gave a strangled moan and pitched headlong down the stairs.

Jo reacted instantly. Dropping her bag, she raced across the pavement and fell to her knees beside the old man. He was gasping desperately and his face was an ominous purple colour. Swiftly Jo felt for his carotid pulse and found it rapid and irregular. He was lying sprawled on his side, so she turned him over and examined his pupils, but even as she looked they suddenly becamed fixed and dilated. His gasping ceased abruptly.

'Oh, no!' cried Jo. 'Oh, no!'

Urgently she checked his respiratory status, but she could no longer see any chest movements, and when she laid her cheek near his mouth there was no tell-tale current of expired air. By now a crowd of curious onlookers had gathered, and Jo glanced up sharply.

'One of you go and call an ambulance at once!' she ordered. 'This man is in cardiac arrest. Can anyone here to mouth-to-mouth resuscitation?'

A young man with the deep suntan and bleached hair of a surfer stepped forward.

'Good,' said Jo. 'Now the rest of you stand back and give us room to work.'

With her fingertips Jo felt for the end of the old man's

breastbone to locate the right point for external cardiac massage. As the surfer tilted back Tom's head and pinched his nostrils shut before blowing into his open mouth, Jo set to work determinedly. Placing her hands palm down one on top of the other, she pumped vigorously, keeping up a steady rate of three compressions to each breath.

'Come on, Tom! Come on!' she urged.

For three or four long minutes there was no response. Then the surfer paused for a moment, and to Jo's jubilation she saw the old man's chest rise and fall of its own accord. Slipping her fingers into the hollow of his throat, she felt a pulse beat, faint but determined.

'Well, glory be!' she cried joyfully. 'I think we've done it!'

By the time the ambulance arrived five minutes later the old man was breathing steadily by himself, although he was still unconscious. But before long the ambulance men had everything under control, and Jo was able to scramble to her feet and take a long, shaky breath. She realised, without really caring, that her tights were laddered and her cream suit was dusty and crumpled. But what did that matter if somebody's life had been saved?

'Are you coming to the hospital with us, miss? We'll be leaving in a moment.'

The ambulance officer's voice cut into her thoughts.

'I can't, I have an interview. . .' she began.

And then stopped. Who am I kidding? she thought despairingly. I can't possibly go to a job interview looking like this. Anyway, it's too late. I'd never get there on time. Better to go with poor old Tom.

'Yes, of course. I'll just grab my bag!' she exclaimed.

She bounded lightly across the pavement to the spot where she had left it. But the moment she reached the bus stop she faltered in mid stride.

'Oh, no!' she groaned.

'What is it?' asked the ambulance officer.

'My bag's gone!' she said. 'Somebody must have stolen it.'

The triage unit at the St Elizabeth Public Hospital was a high-tech centre of activity. Immediately Tom was rushed in on a trolley from the ambulance the staff on duty sprang into action to assess his condition. Jo stood forgotten in the background as nurses rushed to administer oxygen and set up a cardiograph. Tom's shirt was hastily pulled off so that leads could be attached to his chest and connected up to the cardiograph, then a nurse put a drip into his arm. A moment later the doctor, who had been paged, strode in and looked at the cardiograph. He shook his head uneasily and spoke to one of the nurses.

'I think we'd better have a cardiologist here immediately,' he decided. 'Have Dr Simpson paged for me, please, Nurse.'

When the cardiologist arrived he confirmed that Tom had suffered a heart attack. He ordered him to be transferred to the coronary care unit, and Jo tagged determinedly along. At least until some family member turned up to claim him, she felt responsible for the old man.

In the coronary care unit nine or ten nurses sat at a central console covered with knobs and buttons and screens. All around them were patients hooked up to every conceivable type of monitor. Cardiographs stood next to every bed, and most patients had drips in their arms, while the unconscious ones were also receiving oxygen. Jo watched with relief as Tom was fitted up with all the appropriate equipment, including a ventilator. Once he was comfortably settled, a short, dark-haired nurse of about Jo's own age came over to her and touched her sympathetically on the shoulder.

'I'm Nurse Trudy Harper. May I ask your name, please?' she said.

'Webster. Jo Webster,' replied Jo mechanically, her eyes still on Tom's waxen face.

'Try not to worry about him,' said the nurse. 'He's in good hands now. But if you could just come into the office with me I'll get some admission details from you. It's your grandfather, is it?'

Jo shook her head.

'No, he's a total stranger to me,' she explained. 'I just happened to be standing outside the hotel when he had the heart attack, and I'm a nurse myself, so naturally I went to his aid.'

'You don't know his name or anything, then?' asked Trudy.

Jo shook her head as they went into the office together.

'Not really,' she said. 'I know his first name's Tom, because he was sitting at my table for lunch, but he didn't really tell me much else about himself. Except this his wife's dead, although he does have a nephew. I think he's probably an old-age pensioner.'

Trudy looked baffled.

'Well, he's not carrying any identification,' she said, shaking her head. 'I suppose I'll just have to call the police and see what they can do.'

'He was wearing a jacket,' recalled Jo suddenly. 'He left it behind in the hotel. Perhaps you could check up on that.'

'Good thinking,' agreed Trudy. 'I'll mention that to the police.'

As she reached for the phone, Jo cleared her throat.

'Could you also report my handbag as missing?' she asked apologetically. 'Somebody stole it while I was trying to revive poor old Tom. It's brown leather with a gold clasp.'

'Aren't some people unspeakable?' demanded Trudy. 'Hello? Perth Central Police Station. . .?'

When she had finished her phone call she smiled ruefully at Jo.

'Well, I hope that does some good,' she said. 'Now I

suppose you'd like to be getting home. I can lend you your taxi fare, it that's any help.'

Jo flashed her a grateful smile.

'That's awfully kind of you,' she said. 'But would you mind if I waited a bit longer, at least until Tom regains consciousness or one of his relatives arrives? A heart attack can be very scary, and he might find it reassuring if he recognises my face.'

'Of course,' agreed Trudy. 'I'll make you a cup of coffee, and we'll just have to hope that his nephew shows up soon. I know one thing. He'll be very grateful to you when he does.'

But that was where Nurse Harper was wrong. It was another five hours before Rob Challender arrived, and he was not in the least bit grateful. Jo was sitting by Tom's bed in the coronary unit when the door opened. And, although the room remained as warm as ever, she had the uncomfortable sense that a chill gust of wind had just swept through it. Trudy, looking distinctly flustered, ushered a tall, well-dressed man in his early thirties into the ward. He must have been well over six feet in height, with hair so black that it had a bluish sheen under the overhead lights. His eyes were a deep cornflower blue with ridiculously long, almost girlish lashes. But there was nothing girlish about that face. His features had a cruel, sculpted masculinity that was savage in its intensity and his thick black eyebrows almost met beneath a scowling forehead. He wore a beige safari suit that displayed lean, muscular thighs and powerful forearms which he folded across his chest as he surveyed the room.

'This is Dr Rob Challender, Tom Challender's nephew,' announced Trudy in a failing voice. 'Dr Challender, this is Nurse Jo Webster, whom I was telling you about.'

Dr Challender's gaze flicked over Jo like a whiplash, and he gave only a curt growl of acknowledgement before striding across to Tom's bed. Jo's heart hammered in furious bewilderment. Could this really be Tom's nephew, whom he called Bob, and why on earth was he radiating such a lethal dose of hostility? Surely he didn't blame her in some way for Tom's heart attack? But as Dr Challender leaned over the old man's bed his grim face softened. Jo could scarcely believe the change as she saw tenderness, anxiety and relief flit across his features in rapid succession.

'How is he?' he demanded abruptly, looking up at Trudy.

'Dr Simpson is very satisfied with him,' replied Trudy. 'If you'd like to just wait a moment, Dr Challender, I'll get him to come and speak to you.'

'Thank you,' he replied curtly.

Jo rose to her feet and edged nervously along beside Tom's bed. With fifteen patients in the coronary unit there was little room to spare, and Dr Challender's powerful, masculine presence was making her feel distinctly uncomfortable. Particularly since he was still eyeing her with obvious hostility.

'Well, I'd better go,' she said brightly. 'I just wanted to stay until you arrived so Tom wouldn't feel too lonely if he woke. Give him my best wishes, won't you, Dr Challender? Excuse me, if you could just let me slip past you. . .'

'Sit down.'

The command was so abrupt that Jo almost obeyed it out of pure shock. She darted a swift glance at Dr Challender. Did he actually, miracle of miracles, want to thank her for reviving his uncle?

'I'll deal with you in a moment,' he said coldly.

No. Obviously thanks weren't on the agenda. A slow rage began to simmer in Jo's breast. She didn't expect any rewards for what she had done—after all, it was reward enough to have saved somebody's life—but she certainly did not expect to be treated with rudeness and contempt. She opened her mouth to deliver a stinging reply, but at that moment the cardiologist walked into the ward.

'How do you do? I'm Dr Simpson. I believe you're Mr Challender's nephew. If you'd like to come through to the office I just want to have a few words with you about his condition.'

As the two men ambled away, still talking, Jo saw her chance to escape. With a swift farewell to Trudy she marched out of the ward with her head held high. The office door was still half open and she heard the words 'sub endocardial infarction' before she found herself out of earshot. She was halfway down the corridor in the other direction, when suddenly footsteps came loping after her, and a powerful hand descended on her shoulder.

'Wait! I want to talk to you.'

An extraordinary sensation shot through Jo's entire body as Rob Challender swung her round to face him. She was prepared for the anger that raced through her, but not for the adrenalin surge that was almost like a frenzy of excitement as she saw those furious blue eyes glittering down at her. For one insane moment she wondered how it would feel if this dark-haired, seething stranger swept her into his arms and kissed her. Her heart pounded violently.

'I don't think I have anything to say to you, Dr Challender,' she said with a tremor in her voice.

'Oh, but I have something to say to you,' he replied softly.

The voice was like velvet. Low, husky, vibrant. In different circumstances it would have been unbearably seductive, but here in this gleaming hospital corridor it simply filled Jo with an obscure panic. When Dr Challender escorted her back to the office and ushered her inside, Jo was too unnerved to resist.

'Well, how much do you want?' he demanded.

'I—I beg your pardon?' stammered Jo.

'You heard me,' he growled. 'How much?'

Jo's eyes widened. Was this man insane? Was he simply masquerading as a doctor, and in reality quite unbalanced? But there was nothing unbalanced about the look he gave her. It was cool, appraising, deeply contemptuous.

'Well?' he insisted.

'I'm sorry,' snapped Jo. 'I haven't the faintest idea what you're talking about.'

'Oh, come on! My good girl, you're not going to tell me you waited around for five hours in a public hospital just so you could hear me make a pretty little speech of gratitude, are you? Well, I *am* grateful as it happens, but I'd prefer you to cut out the play-acting and just tell me how much you want for saving my uncle's life.'

'Are you insane?' demanded Jo bluntly.

Rob Challender gave a low, savage laugh.

'No,' he retorted. 'But I'm not exactly naïve either. Good God, you must have thought all your Christmases had come at once when Tom Challender, one of the wealthiest men in Western Australia, had a heart attack right at your feet!'

'What?' echoed Jo in astonishment. 'Did you say one of the wealthiest men in Western Australia?'

'Oh, don't play the simpering fool with me!' snapped Rob impatiently. 'Why else would you have been trying to pick him up in the pub, if you didn't know who he was?'

'Pick him up?' cried Jo in outrage. 'How dare you?'

'Oh, yes, I like the injured innocence! You do it so well I could almost believe it. But I've spoken to the barmaid on the telephone, and she saw you kissing him in the public lounge. You don't seriously think you're the first grasping little schemer who has thought she could get her hooks into a lonely old man, do you? You women make me sick! Or do you really expect me to believe that you didn't know who he was?'

'I don't expect you to believe anything, Dr Challender!' said Jo in a voice shaking with rage. 'In fact, it is a matter of complete indifference to me what you believe. I had no idea who your uncle was. I thought he was an old-age pensioner, and his name means nothing to me even now.'

'What?' demanded Rob mockingly. 'You've never heard of Tom Challender, the reclusive mining magnate, who discovered one of the richest goldfields in Western Australia?'

'No, I have not! But I've met a sweet old man whom I knew only as Tom, who thought the sun shone out of his nephew Bob, and I can tell you this. Tom Challender may know a lot about mining, but he's a hell of a judge of character. Now, if you'll excuse me, I've been insulted enough. I'm leaving!'

Jo leapt to her feet and marched towards the door, but Rob was already barring her way. His powerful frame towered over her, as immovable and granite-hard as a cliff-face. One lean, brown hand closed over her wrist.

'Wait,' he ordered, scanning her face with those searing blue eyes. 'Maybe I've been a bit too hard on you.'

'Maybe?' she squeaked in outrage. 'Let me past, damn you!'

He fended her off as easily as if she were a kitten. Amusement was beginning to replace the suspicion in his eyes.

'Look,' he said slowly. 'I really am very grateful for what you did. There's no question that you saved my uncle's life. I'd genuinely like you to accept something from me. Shall we say a thousand dollars?'

He reached into his breast pocket and took out a wad of silver-coloured notes, which he pressed into Jo's hand. Her mouth hardened. Then, with a swift, satisfying movement, she tore them across once, twice, three times, and threw the pieces fluttering into the air.

'Thank you for your generosity, Dr Challender!' she

said through clenched teeth. 'Now will you kindly let me pass?'

At that moment Trudy Harper tapped at the office door and then came in. Seizing her opportunity, Jo hurried out the open door and stormed down the corridor with her lips set and her head held high. With a muffled curse, Rob Challender hurried after her. Bewildered and dismayed, Trudy stared after them and then looked down at the confetti of torn bank notes on the floor.

'Wait!' she cried. 'What's all this money? What am I to do with it?'

'Stick it together and give it to the hospital building fund!' shouted Rob as he raced after Jo.

He caught her up in the lift, but it was full of other people, so neither of them said anything. Smouldering amber eyes met icy blue ones, and Jo tossed her head and turned away to stare pointedly at an advertisement for surgical prostheses. The moment they reached the ground floor Jo hurried out with the rest of the crowd, intent on leaving Rob Challender for dead. But he was too quick for her. As she emerged on to the pavement outside the hospital, his hand closed over her wrist.

'Stop!' he ordered. 'I need to talk to you.'

'You already did!' she retorted, marching away.

It wasn't an easy task with over six feet of extremely resistant male attached to her wrist.

'Where are you going?' he demanded.

'Home!' she snapped.

'Where's that?'

'Subiaco,' she replied, heading purposefully down the street, with Rob still attached.

'That's miles from here. And anyway, you're heading in the wrong direction. Let me give you a lift.'

'I'd sooner get in a car with a tiger snake!' cried Jo.

He pulled her up sharply at that, so that she was suddenly aware of the immense strength in that lean brown hand. His blue eyes gazed searchingly down at her.

'Look, I'm sorry if I insulted you earlier on,' he said sincerely. 'I've had good reason in the past to be wary of fortune-hunters around my uncle, but myabe I was wrong about you. I'm not trying to give you a hard time now. All I want to do is see that you get safely home.'

Jo hesitated, half swayed by those intent blue eyes. But the word 'maybe' sent a slow fire burning through her.

'I'm a big girl!' she retorted. 'I can look after myself, thank you, Dr Challender!'

His eyes hardened at the anger in her voice.

'Can you?' he parried. 'When you don't even know which direction is the way home?'

'I'll find it on my map!' cried Jo. 'At least. . . I would, except the map was in my bag, and my bag's been stolen. Oh, hell, what a day!'

She was suddenly overcome by a wave of exhaustion and despair. Raising her free hand, she pushed her tumbled hair out of her eyes and bit her lip. It was all she could do not to burst into tears.

'Miss Webster? Are you all right?'

His voice was suddenly full of concern, and somehow that seemed to bring Jo even closer to tears. She responded with a brittle gaiety.

'I'm fine,' she babbled. 'My clothes are filthy, my tights are ripped, my bag's been stolen with all my money and job certificates in it, I've just spent five hours in a hospital with nothing but a cup of instant coffee and then been accused of being a gold-digger, but I am absolutely, wonderfully, terrifically, totally fine! Now leave me alone, will you?'

'Don't be ridiculous!' said Rob. 'I'm driving you home. Come on, my car's in the hospital car park over there.'

He seized her by the shoulders and propelled her towards the car park. Taken by surprise, Jo walked the first two steps, and then stopped in her tracks and refused to budge.

'I am not going anywhere with you!' she stated in a smouldering voice. 'Now will you kindly get out of here?'

'No, I won't!' exclaimed Rob roughly. 'For God's sake, what do you take me for? You've no money for a taxi, and it's after eight o'clock at night. Perth is pretty safe as cities go, but I'm certainly not leaving you to walk miles along the riverbank alone. Now get in my car!'

'Stop bossing me about!' shouted Jo.

'I will as soon as you do what you're told!' roared Rob.

Jo paused, staring at him mutinously. Then her lips twitched. 'That is the most ridiculous statement I've heard in a long time!' she pointed out.

Rob smiled too. A surprisingly engaging smile that made his rather forbidding features relax into charm and warmth.

'Suppose we call a truce and get you safely home?' he suggested.

Jo hesitated a moment longer, then gave in. A slow sigh escaped her. 'All right,' she agreed.

'What's your address?'

'Twenty-eight, Winterbourne Avenue, Subiaco,' she replied.

'We're on our way,' said Rob.

As the car purred out of the car park Jo relaxed against the upholstery with another deep sigh. It had been a long day, and she was content simply to enjoy the comfort of luxuriously upholstered seats, soothing classical music on the stereo and the panorama of Perth by night slipping past the windows. The sky was a velvety dark blue, and the bright city lights gleamed red and orange and green and white from shop-fronts and cinemas and nightclubs. Before long the car took a turn and they came out on the road leading along the river front. A vast expanse of tranquil dark water flowed between them and the opposite bank. Jo took a quick, appreciative breath.

'I can't get over how beautiful the Swan River is,' she murmured wonderingly. 'It's nearly as good as the Harbour back home.'

'You're not a local girl, then?' asked Rob.

'No, I'm from Sydney. I'm here on a working holiday. But you're a genuine native of Perth, I assume?'

'Born and bred,' confirmed Rob. 'Although I spend most of my time these days at Rainbow End.'

He gave a faint sigh.

'Rainbow End?' queried Jo.

'It's a mining town about an hour's flight from Perth,' explained Rob. 'Tom actually founded it and named it back in the early fifties. The population's about five thousand now, and it's as pleasant as you can reasonably expect for a mining community dumped in the middle of a semi desert.'

'But you'd rather be in Perth?' Jo hazarded a guess.

Rob gave a low, rueful chuckle. 'Yes,' he admitted.

'What do you do there?' asked Jo. 'Are you involved in the mining administration?'

'No,' said Rob in a subdued voice. 'Although I think I would be if Tom had his way. No, I'm one of the local GPs at the mine's health centre.'

'You don't sound entirely happy about that,' remarked Jo thoughtfully.

Rob shrugged, staring down the bright lights of the road ahead.

'Are people ever entirely happy with their lives?' he countered. 'How about you? You said you were on a working holiday. So what are you doing exactly?'

'Nothing so far,' admitted Jo. 'I've only been in Perth for a week or so, but I was hoping to get a job at the St Jude's Children's Hospital. I was on the way to the interview today when I met Tom.'

Rob gave a soft whistle.

'So you've missed out on your chances of a job through all this?' he asked.

'I don't know,' sighed Jo. 'I tried to phone from the

hospital this afternoon, but I couldn't get through. I'll ring again tomorrow morning. Perhaps I'll be lucky.'

At that moment Rob took a turn and swung the car smoothly into a lane that led across the river.

'You're going the wrong way!' said Jo sharply. 'Subiaco's on this side of the river.'

'I know,' replied Rob. 'But I thought the least I could do was give you some dinner on the way home. You must be starving. And I flew down from Rainbow End when I heard the news about Tom, so I've had nothing to eat this afternoon either. What do you say?'

'But my clothes are all torn and soiled,' protested Jo. 'I can't go anywhere looking like this.'

'Don't worry,' Rob reassured her. 'The people know me at this place. They'd let you in if you were wearing a G-string.'

Jo cast him a resentful glance which made him chuckle appreciatively. But common sense told her he was right. Mary Lou could hardly be expected to keep dinner for her until nine o'clock, and she was hungry.

'All right,' she agreed ungraciously.

The restaurant was set right on the edge of the river in the suburb of Apple Cross, and Jo soon saw that Rob was right about the G-string. A waiter came gliding respectfully across the floor to meet them, and guided them to a table by the window overlooking the water. With courteous skill he pulled back her chair, and then spread a snowy napkin across her lap. If he had noticed the large hole in the knee of Jo's tights he gave no sign of it, and his voice was almost reverent as he addressed her.

'A pleasant evening, madam. Can I get you both something to drink?'

Rob looked questioningly at Jo.

'A small gin and tonic, please,' she murmured.

'Very good, madam. And you, sir?'

'Scotch and water. So what made you choose Perth for your working holiday?'

Rob sat back in his chair and surveyed Jo thought-fully across the table. It was a very attractive table, covered in a plum-coloured cloth with an ornate arrange-ment of frangipani and asparagus fern in the centre, flanked by two slender cream candles in crystal holders. The rest of the room was dimly lit, and the candlelight winked back from the polished silver cutlery and the gold borders of the Wedgwood plates. In the back-ground a pianist in a dazzling white shirt and black tails sat playing a rippling Chopin piano sonata. It was the sort of restaurant where lovers might meet for a quiet, romantic dinner. Very wealthy lovers. Jo, who was accustomed to dining in much humbler surround-ings, felt suddenly overwhelmed.

'I. . . Sorry?' she said.

'I asked you why you chose Perth for your working holiday,' repeated Rob with a touch of impatience.

Jo shrugged.

'No special reason,' she admitted. 'Except that my closest friend Mary Lou Fowler, who trained with me, married and settled here several years ago. She's been pestering me for ages to come and visit her. And this seemed like a good time to do it.'

'Oh, why's that?' asked Rob, picking up the glass which the wine waiter had just set in front of him. 'Cheers.'

'Cheers,' agreed Jo mechanically, sipping at her gin and tonic. Its bitter, refreshing flavour was welcome after the rigours of the day, and she was not even aware that she sighed before she spoke. 'My father has just remarried.'

'And you're not too happy about it?' probed Rob gently.

Jo cast him a swift, shame-faced glance.

'Something like that,' she admitted. 'It's stupid for a woman of my age, I know, but I still don't like to see my mother being replaced. My stepmother is nice enough, and it's eight years since my mother died, but somehow

I hate to see all her bits and pieces being thrown out or rearranged. I'd been planning to take a holiday for years, so this seemed like a good time to take the plunge.'

'You were very close to your mother, then?' asked Rob sympathetically.

'Yes, I was. She died of cancer when I was nineteen. I took a year off my training to nurse her, so I was there at the very end. . .'

She bit her lip, unable to go on. To her surprise, Rob's warm fingers closed over hers.

'That must have been hard for you,' he said softly. 'It's a diabolical illness. But still, you were fortunate to have her for so long. I scarcely knew my parents.'

Jo looked enquiringly at him as he released her hand.

'They died in an accident at the mine when I was five years old,' he explained soberly. 'I only have the haziest memories of them, and I've always envied people who had a normal family life. Tom and Bet brought me up, and they were wonderful to me, but it wasn't quite the same.'

Jo's lips curved into a reminiscent smile.

'Tom seems to be quite a character,' she remarked.

'Oh, he is,' agreed Rob. 'A great old bloke, but as obstinate as they come.'

At that moment another waiter appeared with a pair of menus in ornate, Florentine leather covers. There was silence as they both perused the mouthwatering list of dishes.

'Well?' asked Rob at last. 'Any thoughts on the subject of food?'

'Just a small helping of fettuccine with a side salad, thanks,' said Jo. 'I had a rather substantial lunch today.'

'Well, I didn't,' said Rob emphatically. 'So I'll go for broke, if you don't mind. Smoked salmon pâté, carpet bag steak and a large slice of pavlova. With crackers and cheese to follow. I had a hard day's work.'

Jo grinned. 'A very hard day, by the sound of it,' she commented.

Rob smiled. 'You'd better believe it,' he said. 'A jeep overturned near the tailings dump with two men trapped inside it. Fortunately neither of them was seriously injured, but it took us over an hour to cut them free, and the temperature was forty-seven degrees Centigrade in the shade. So I think I've earned my dinner.'

He gave the orders to the waiter, and handed back the two menus with a smiling comment with made both men chuckle. Rob had a throaty, infectious laugh, and Jo was suddenly stunned by the contrast with the ogre who had terrorised her earlier in the evening. Perhaps she had been wrong about Rob Challender, she decided generously. Perhaps he was a thoroughly nice man at heart.

As the evening wore on this impression was confirmed. Now that his initial hostility had worn off Rob proved to be a remarkably sympathetic listener. Jo found herself telling him about her passionate commitment to nursing sick children, about her feelings of inadequacy and grief whenever a child patient died, about the compensating rewards when sick kids recovered. In return Rob chatted easily to her about cinema and yachting and medical techniques and, when she had finished her last delicious mouthful of fettuccine, he even succeeded in coaxing her on to the dance-floor.

'I can't,' protested Jo in a low, anxious voice, as she looked down at the black smudges on her sleeve and the hole in her tights. 'People will stare at me.'

'Let them,' said Rob carelessly. 'If you always worry about what people think you'll never do what you really want to.'

So Jo gave in and allowed herself to be coaxed out on to the dance-floor. The pianist had gone from Chopin sonatas to Strauss waltzes, and Rob whirled her around the floor as lightly as if they were floating six inches above it. He was a magical dancer, and Jo had a moment's pure bliss as she heard the music surging and lilting about her and felt Rob's strong fingers pressed against her back. She could not help but be aware of his raw, untamed masculinity, of the faint pressure of his cheek against her curls, of the warm, powerful strength of his body against hers. For a few, delirious, intoxicating minutes she wondered what it would be like if they really had come here as lovers instead of antagonists who had met by pure chance. Then the music stopped, and Rob led her back to her seat. Breathless and smiling, she glanced up at him as he pulled her chair back for her.

'Thank you,' she said sincerely. 'I enjoyed that.'

'So did I,' he agreed.

He sounded slightly surprised. His eyes met hers, and a quick flush of colour rushed into her cheeks. She was acutely conscious of the fact that his right hand was resting against her shoulder, and the contact seemed to send quivers darting through her entire body. Perhaps Rob was aware of this odd fact too, for he made no move to push the chair in, but simply stood staring down at her. Then the spell was broken.

'Hello, Rob,' cooed a sultry female voice.

Jo started, and Rob spun round as a tall, glamorous brunette materialised at his elbow. His face lit up, and Jo felt a stab of something suspiciously like jealousy as she saw the expression on his face.

'Miranda!' he exclaimed joyfully.

Jo craned her neck shamelessly for a better look, and saw an elegant siren in a silvery, glittering evening dress that left her creamy shoulders and bosom blatantly exposed. She was leaning seductively on the arm of an equally tall and handsome man, whose face seemed tantalisingly familiar to Jo.

'You remember Stephen, don't you, darling?' she asked.

Rob's face was frankly hostile as he gave the newcomer a cool nod.

'Hello, Stephen,' he said. 'I don't think either of you have met my companion, Jo Webster. Jo, this is Miranda Sinclair and her friend Stephen Lester. Miranda's one of our company lawyers and Stephen is a current-affairs reporter on television. Jo's a nurse.'

'Really? How fascinating!' replied Miranda wearily. 'How do you do?'

'How do you do?' replied Jo in a subdued voice.

'Miranda, I need to talk to you,' began Rob. 'Jo and I have finished eating, and I'll be taking her home in a moment. Are you going back to your place now?'

Miranda gave a little trill of laughter.

'Sorry, Rob,' she said sweetly. 'Steve and I are going on to a nightclub. Victoire's actually.'

Rob frowned. 'I thought you were coming to Victoire's with me tonight,' he said with obvious annoyance.

Miranda's exquisite features tensed into a sulky pout.

'It wasn't a firm date,' she countered. 'And in any case, darling, you're the one who stood me up. Mention was made of dinner too, if I remember correctly, but there wasn't a sign of you by seven-thirty, so I assumed you weren't coming.'

'I tried to call and let you know,' protested Rob. 'But you phone was off the hook. Tom had a heart attack.'

A gleam of something suspiciously like excitement lit Miranda's lustrous dark eyes, but her voice was suitably hushed and sympathetic.

'Oh, Rob, no! Poor old Tom! Not fatal, I hope?'

'Of course not!' retorted Rob irritably. 'I'd hardly be sitting here if he were dead, would I? But bad enough, all the same. He collapsed in the street and stopped breathing. Fortunately Jo was able to come to his aid and revive him.'

'Really?' marvelled Miranda. 'I suppose that's how you ruined your clothes, then?'

Her gaze flickered insultingly over Jo's cream suit, and came to rest on the large smear of dirt that disfigured the sleeve.

'Yes,' replied Jo bluntly.

Something about Miranda's mocking expression was making her blood pressure rise steadily. Does she think

I wear filthy clothes all the time? thought Jo furiously. But she said nothing.

'What a pity,' murmured Miranda. 'Still, it's lucky you weren't wearing anything good, isn't it?'

Jo bit her lip at this casual dismissal of her best suit, and felt a slow rage begin to simmer inside her. At that instant she felt she could have cheerfully strangled Miranda.

'Well,' said Miranda, leaning her head briefly against Stephen's shoulder, 'Come on, Steve. Chop, chop! We'll miss the start of the floor show if we don't hurry. Do give me a call next time you're in Perth, won't you, Rob?'

She raised one beautifully manicured hand and blew a tantalising kiss to Rob as she went gliding away. Thoroughly nauseated by this coyness, Jo cast a swift glance at Rob, expecting to share a sardonic smile. But to her amazement he was gazing after Miranda with an expression of mixed rage and longing on his face. As Jo watched, he shook his head slightly like a man coming up from under water.

'Have you finished your coffee?' he asked. 'Would you like to go?'

'Yes, please.'

Jo became aware that her body was aching in the oddest places. She had hit her knee quite hard as she'd flung herself on the pavement to treat Tom, and her wrists were sore from the effort of giving cardio-pulmonary massage. Even the fold-out couch-bed at Mary Lou's was beginning to seem like a tempting place to be.

As the waiter bowed them respectfully out of the tinted glass entrance doors of the restaurant, Jo stole a quick glance at her companion. It didn't need a clairvoyant to see that Rob was extremely annoyed about something. His lips were set in a grim line and his eyes looked even stormier than when he had first confronted Jo at the hospital. Taking out his car key, he opened Jo's door and then strode around to his own side of the vehicle. Jo winced as his door slammed shut, and he started the engine with a crash of gears and a burst of speed that made the tyres squeal protestingly.

'Do you always drive this badly?' she asked without thinking, as the car lurched out on to the open road.

'No, I do not,' ground out Rob. 'Do you always say the first thing that comes into your head no matter how tactless it is?'

Jo thought about that.

'Yes, I'm afraid I do,' she admitted ruefully. 'Act first, think later, that's me. But I'm sorry if I offended you.'

Rob chuckled mirthlessly.

'Never mind,' he said. 'At least it's better than calculating every damned twitch of your eyebrow the way some women do. Now I'd better get into the right lane for Subiaco.'

Jo was startled to find that her watch showed just after midnight as the car purred gently up the tree-lined street to Mary Lou's house. Most of the houses were already in darkness, but Mary Lou had left a light burning on the front porch for Jo.

'I'll see you to the door,' said Rob.

'There's no need,' began Jo, but he was already out of the car, opening her door and then hauling open the sagging iron gate.

'We'd better go quietly,' whispered Jo. 'I don't want to wake the children.'

'Fine,' agreed Rob with a conspiratorial wink. With exaggerated care they tiptoed side by side up the uneven stone pathway. But just as they reached the front steps Jo put her foot on a toy tip-truck that lay half concealed under an overhanging grevillea bush. With a muffled shriek she flailed her arms in a desperate attempt to regain her balance, and then fell. Rob's hands seemed to come from nowhere. He caught her just before she hit the ground, and the full softness of her breast brushed against the taut muscles of his arm. She heard his swift intake of breath, then he drew her to her feet.

'I'm sorry,' he began. 'I didn't intend——'

'I know,' cut in Jo hastily.

He was still holding her by the arms when her hair, which had been swept up in a loose chignon, suddenly rebelled and tumbled free. It fell gloriously around her shoulders in a wild mass of tawny-brown curls which caught the light from the porch and gleamed like copper. Without even thinking Rob picked up a tawny strand and tidied it back from Jo's face.

'You have magnificent hair,' he said.

'Thank you,' replied Jo huskily.

For some reason she felt oddly breathless, and she took a quick gulp of air. Her shoulders heaved with the movement, and she found that Rob was looking down at her intently. A thrill of pure insanity went through her. I wish he'd kiss me, she thought with a strange, pulsing ache that seemed to pierce right through her. And then, to her amazement, he did exactly that. His arms tightened around her and his mouth came down on hers. It was a long, throbbing kiss that sent shivers of excitement coursing through Jo's entire body. Nobody had ever kissed her as Rob Challender was doing now, and she responded with all the recklessness of an impulsive nature. For thirty blissful seconds they stood locked in each other's arms, oblivious to everything around them. Then abruptly sanity returned.

'How dare you?' exclaimed Jo, pushing him away and struggling free. She was furious with herself for her momentary lapse, but it was Rob whom she blamed. 'How could you? Don't you have any principles at all, to take advantage of a woman like that?'

Her whole body was tense with rage. Her tawny eyes flashed, and even her bronze hair seemed to flame and crackle in the lamplight. Rob stepped back a pace, but his lips tightened contemptuously.

'You seemed willing enough a moment ago,' he pointed out.

'Willing!' cried Jo, stung by this simple truth. 'You *would* choose to think that, wouldn't you?'

Rob ran his fingers through his glossy dark hair, and sighed impatiently.

'You women are all the same!' he exclaimed angrily. 'You lead a man on and then slam the door in his face. Well, don't worry. No! You won't have to bother with my company again.'

'Fine with me!' retorted Jo, retreating up the stairs to the front door. 'Because let me tell you this. If I never see you again, Rob Challender, it'll still be too soon for me! So goodnight and thanks for a wonderful evening!'

CHAPTER TWO

'Jo! TELEPHONE for you!'

Mary Lou came hurrying down the garden to the sandpit, where Jo was building a fort with the two little Fowler boys. In spite of herself Jo felt her pulses race as the image of Rob Challender leapt into her mind.

'Who is it? Do you know?' she asked a trifle breathlessly.

Mary Lou shrugged.

'Somebody called Gavin Lyall,' she replied, scooping up one of her sons. 'Don't put that horrid beetle in your mouth, Paul! Sorry, Jo! I didn't recognise the name. Does it mean anything to you?'

'No,' admitted Jo, scraping sand off her shoes. 'But it might be somebody from St Jude's. They told me they'd filled all the vacancies the day of the interview, but they put me on a waiting list and promised to call me as soon as they had something. So keep your fingers crossed for me!'

As she hurried up the garden she gave herself a mental shake. You are disgraceful, Jo Webster, she told herself sternly. It's three days since you met Rob Challender, you couldn't stand the man, and yet here you are jumping like a teenage girl every time the phone rings! Just because of a kiss that didn't mean a thing. Now calm down and start thinking about something important like getting a job.

'Hello,' said Jo cautiously, lifting the receiver. 'This is Josephine Webster speaking.'

'G'day, love.'

The voice was no more than a whispered thread, but it made Jo's heart leap with joy.

'Tom! she cried. 'How lovely to hear from you! How are you getting on?'

'Right as rain, thanks to you,' said the old man stoutly. 'No good complainin' anyway. They don't take no notice of me when I do. Listen, love. I just rung to say thank you and to ask you something. Have you got a minute?'

'Yes, of course,' agreed Jo in bewilderment. 'But Mary Lou said somebody called Gavin Lyall was on the phone. . .'

There was a low chuckle at the other end of the line.

'Yes,' agreed Tom. 'That's the flamin' quack that's treatin' me, but I decided to do me own askin'. Now look, love, I hear you missed out on that job nursin' the kiddies because you was too tied up with me. Is that right?'

'Yes,' admitted Jo reluctantly. 'But don't you give it another thought, Tom. I was only thankful that I was able to help you.'

'Well, Gawd bless you for sayin' so, love,' replied Tom. 'But what I want to know is this. Have you got another job yet?'

'No,' said Jo. 'But St Jude's have put me on their waiting list. So there could be something any day now——'

'Any day is no bloody use when you need money in your pocket right now,' cut in Tom decisively. 'All right, well that settles it, then. I've got a job for you. You can come and nurse me.'

'What?' exclaimed Jo incredulously.

A wheezy chuckle came gusting down the line.

'I thought that ud make yer sit up and take notice,' said Tom with satisfaction. 'Well, will you do it?'

'But. . .do what?' asked Jo in bewilderment.

Tom sighed.

'Look, love,' he said seriously. 'I'm on borrowed time now. We all know that, and it's no use beatin' about the bush. But I want to get me affairs in order. Get back to Rainbow End one last time, make sure all me people at the mine are OK, get things ship-shape to hand over to young Bob, tie up all the loose ends. The trouble is that me doctor here is too big for his boots. Says he won't let me out of hospital unless I've got a nurse runnin' round like a nanny with me wherever I go. So I want you to do it, Jo.'

Jo gathered her straying wits.

'But, Tom, I'm a children's nurse,' she protested. 'There must be hundreds of nurses in Western Australia better qualified in geriatrics——'

'I don't want them. I want you,' insisted Tom stubbornly.

'Well——' began Jo.

'Aw, come on,' wheedled Tom. 'You wouldn't deny a pore old man his last wish, would you?'

Jo burst out laughing.

'Tom, you are quite shameless!' she reproved.

Tom chuckled too.

'It's no good gettin' old if you don't get cunning!' he retorted. 'Come on, love. Will you at least come in and talk to Lyall about it? They've moved me outa the public hospital, you know, and I'm in one of them posh clinics at Dalkeith now. It's not far from where you're stayin', and I can send a car for you.'

In spite of the bravado there was a pleading undertone in the old man's voice, and Jo's soft heart was touched. Tears pricked the back of her eyes.

'How can I refuse?' she replied. 'I'll come this morning.'

Gavin Lyall, the cardiologist who was treating Tom, proved to be a red-faced, greying man in his late fifties. After Jo had paid a brief visit to the old man Dr Lyall ushered her into his office.

'Please sit down, Miss Webster,' he invited, waving her into a chair. 'Now, I understand Mr Challender wants to employ you as his private nurse. . .' He put on his spectacles, thrust aside a litter of papers, and peered thoughtfully at a manila folder. 'How do you feel about that?'

Jo shifted uncomfortably as Dr Lyall suddenly transfixed her with his piercing blue gaze.

'I have mixed feelings about it,' she admitted. 'I like Tom very much, and I'd like to help him out, but I have my doubts whether I'm the right person to do it. I did a bit of geriatrics in my basic training, of course, but most of my work since I qualified has been in large city hospitals. Accident and emergency, obstetrics, paediatrics, that sort of thing. It doesn't really seem the most appropriate background for this sort of work.'

'Do you have any of your nursing certificates with you?' asked Dr Lyall.

'Yes,' agreed Jo, handing a sheaf of papers across the desk. 'I'm sorry they're a bit dirty and crumpled. My handbag was stolen a few days ago, and these were in it at the time. Whoever was responsible simply grabbed my purse and tossed everything else on the floor of a public lavatory. The police only found it yesterday.'

Dr Lyall winced.

'That's back luck,' he said sympathetically, as his gaze skimmed over the documents. 'Nevertheless, your qualifications are very impressive. General training and accident and emergency at Royal North Shore, then a stint at Crown Street to do your obstetrics. Then on to Camperdown for paediatrics. You're a very accomplished young lady.'

'Thank you,' murmured Jo.

'But are you willing to tackle the task of nursing Tom Challender?' continued Dr Lyall.

Jo hesitated.

'I can't help feeling that he might be better off with somebody more experienced at private nursing,' she admitted frankly.

'Nevertheless, he wants you,' countered Dr Lyall, looking at Jo over the top of his spectacles. 'And, having met you, I'm inclined to think he's right.'

'I beg your pardon?' replied Jo, startled.

Dr Lyall sighed humorously.

'I like to think I'm Tom's friend as well as his doctor,' he said. 'And I know from past experience that he's a stubborn old bloke. Once he takes a notion into his head, you can't shift him from it. And he's determined that he wants you to nurse him. In my view the fact that you're none too keen on the idea is probably a good thing. You're not likely to see the job simply as a chance to line your pockets.'

Jo looked horrified. 'Of course not!' she exclaimed. 'As if anybody would!'

Dr Lyall frowned. 'You'd be surprised how some people are affected by money,' he said. 'But, however rich Tom Challender may be, he's also just a lonely, frightened old man facing the prospect of death. And, as his doctor, I'd like you to help him through that, if you feel you can.'

Jo swallowed, fighting down a sudden rush of emotion. But her voice was cool and professional when she replied.

'What exactly is involved in the job, Doctor?' she asked.

'Well, now,' explained Dr Lyall. 'What it amounts to is this. Tom suffered a sub endocardial infarction the other day, and the cardiograph revealed that it wasn't the first by any means. The heart muscle shows signs of damage from previous attacks and, as if that weren't bad enough, he's suffering from severe hypertension. His blood pressure on arrival in hospital was a hundred and ninety over a hundred and thirty. To put it bluntly, he could pop off at any moment. However, if we could bring his blood pressure down dramatically he might coast along for a few years yet. As it happens, we have a new drug that's been very promising in reducing hypertension, and I'd like to try it on Tom. But he's already made up his mind that he won't stay in hospital a minute longer than he has to. In fact he's threatening to discharge himself this afternoon and fly back to Rainbow

End. Now, if I had a competent nurse to administer the drug and monitor his blood pressure on a daily basis I'd be happy to let him out in, say, another week's time. But if the old coot goes today without anyone to take care of him he'll probably be signing his own death warrant. I think you'd find the job pleasant enough. He's offering an excellent salary, you'd be in luxury accommodation at Rainbow End, and all you'd have to do basically would be administer the tablets and monitor his blood pressure.'

'So I'd really just be sitting around for an indefinite period doing nothing most of the time?' demanded Jo.

Dr Lyall laughed aloud at the miserable expression on her face.

'There are plenty of people who would jump at the chance to do exactly that,' he pointed out. 'But I can see you're a girl who thrives on being busy. I'll tell you what. Would you feel any better about the job if you were allowed to help out at the mine's medical centre? It's only a stone's throw away from Tom's house, and I'd have no objection to the idea. We can put a medical-alert button on him so that he can buzz you if he needs help. And, of course, you'd be near him at night time, which is another thing I'm concerned about. Would that suit you?'

Jo turned the idea over in her mind.

'I think it probably would,' she said doubtfully. 'But it's rather hard to judge when I haven't seen the facilities at Rainbow End or anything. . .'

'No problem,' replied Dr Lyall. 'We can send you up by plane this afternoon, you can look the place over, and tell us your decision. And, if you like, we could make the initial appointment just for a month until Tom comes back for a full cardiac check-up. At that time we could review the situation, and see how you felt about continuing in the job. How does that sound?'

Jo looked startled. Fly five hundred miles just to take

a look at the place? When she might only be nursing Tom for a month anyway?

'F-fine,' she stammered.

'Good,' said Dr Lyall crisply. 'Let's go and tell the news to Tom, shall we?'

When they entered the luxurious private ward they found the frail old man propped up against a pile of pillows chatting to a visitor. But Jo's numb brain barely registered that Tom's cheeks now showed a faint tinge of colour or that his blue eyes were alert and lively. For her entire being was focused on the man who stood next to the bed. Seeing that tall, powerful figure with the raven dark hair and the sardonic face seemed to rivet her to the spot. She found that her heart was beating faster. Her gaze slid down to the lean, brown fingers resting on the bed head and she had an unwilling flash of memory about how wonderful they had felt as Rob had caressed her hair. He turned, and their eyes met. The mockery in his face showed her that he was sharing the same memory, and colour flooded her cheeks.

'Miss Webster, this is Dr Rob Challender. Tom's nephew,' said Dr Lyall.

'We've already. . .met,' murmured Rob in a throaty voice.

Jo squirmed. Not only met, but touched, kissed, flowed together like molten lava, she thought with a pang. How could I have been so stupid?

'That's real nice,' said Tom weakly from his bed. 'And they got on like a house on fire, didn't you love? Bob's been tellin' me all about it. How you fell over the toy truck an' all.'

Jo's eyes met Rob's in sudden alarm, but his faint, warning shake of the head reassured her.

'I told Tom how you had a little fall and I had to treat you for shock,' said Rob smoothly.

'Oh, is that what you were doing?' retorted Jo tartly.

The sudden gleam of amusement in his dark blue eyes

almost made her chuckle, in spite of her annoyance. But Rob now passed on to more important matters.

'Tom's just been telling me that you're advising him to hire a private nurse, Gavin,' he explained. 'That sounds sensible to me. Do you have anybody in mind? I'm sure some of the agencies must have some excellent people on their books with experience in geriatrics and palliative care.'

'Well, actually——' began Dr Lyall, but Tom interrupted.

'Jo's going to do it, aren't you, love?'

Rob's expression, which only a moment before had been amused and almost friendly, suddenly turned into a cold, hostile mask.

'I see,' he said curtly.

'You don't see nothin'. Not even what's in front of your face, most of the time,' cut in Tom. 'Jo likes me and I like her and that's all there is to it. I reckon she can give me me tablets and take me blood pressure just as well as any other nurse, so it's no flamin' use gettin' some pasty-faced biddy with a certificate in Jerry Yatricks or whatever you call it in to deal with me. If I'm gunna die I might as well die in cheerful company and be done with it. Is that clear enough for yer, Bob?'

Jo was surprised and moved to see the spasm of emotion that passed over Rob's face. Then he gave the old man's hand a swift squeeze, and nodded soberly.

'Whatever you want, Tom,' he sighed. 'You're the boss.'

'Good,' said Tom with satisfaction. 'I'm glad we got that straight. Well, will you do it, love?'

Jo was staring at the two Challenders in dismay. The last thing she wanted to do was be caught in a family feud of mammoth proportions. She knew as well as Rob did that her skills were not ideal for the job, and she didn't want to be reminded of the fact every day. But Tom's mute, appealing gaze was hard to resist.

'I'm not sure——' she began.

But Gavin Lyall cut in.

'I thought we'd fly Miss Webster up this afternoon, and let her take a look at Rainbow End,' he suggested. 'Then she can make up her mind whether she wants to stay or not. She's afraid she won't have enough to do, so I've told her she can help out at the mine's medical centre whenever she's not busy with you, Tom.'

'Good idea,' said Tom approvingly. 'There you are, Bob. You'll get a new nurse into the bargain!'

Too late Jo remembered that Rob Challender was the chief GP at the mine's medical centre. Did she really want this cold, unfriendly man with his hostile blue eyes as her new boss? She opened her mouth to gabble a frantic refusal, and caught Tom's wistful gaze.

'What time does the plane leave?' she asked in a sinking voice.

Tom's face lit up.

'You can go with Bob. He's on his way, aren't you, mate?'

Rob nodded, unsmiling.

'There's a commercial flight at three-fifteen p.m.,' he said. 'And I suppose I can bring her back in one of the company's Piper Navajos this evening. I'm due back by eight o'clock anyway to meet Miranda.'

Tom nodded, his eyebrows fluttering wearily.

'Good lad,' he said absent-mindedly. Then a thought struck him.

'You'll be glad of a bit more help at the medical centre, won't you, Bob?' he asked. 'Didn't you say one of your lasses there was off on maternity leave?'

'Yes,' confirmed Rob, nodding his head. 'Pam Morrow. Three babies in three years. I don't know how she does it!'

Tom chuckled.

'I do!' he murmured wickedly. Then he closed his eyes. 'Off you go, you two. I hope you have a good trip and get better acquainted.'

The first half of Tom's wish was certainly fulfilled,

even if the second half wasn't. The flight to Rainbow
End was spectacularly uneventful. Outside the plane
brilliant sunshine lit up the flat landscape with its
endless miles of red dust and scrubby eucalypt trees,
enlivened only by an occasional salt pan or the long,
straight slash of a country road. Not the slightest sign of
air turbulence marred their journey, but Jo could not
quell the turmoil that raged within her. From the
moment they had left the hospital in Perth Rob
Challender had virtually ignored her. And although he
now sat with his muscular, brown thigh almost touching
Jo's blue floral skirt, they might as well have been a
million miles apart for all the attention he paid her. How
on earth could she endure a few hours of this, let alone
several months?

'Excuse me, sir. Could you just pass this tray of
sandwiches to your wife?' asked the air hostess politely.

Jo choked back a grin as Rob scowled blackly and
handed her the tray.

'Thank you, dear,' she said sweetly.

There was no reply, but the scowl intensified.

It was a relief when the plane finally began to lose
height and banked sharply for its approach to the
airfield. Jo pressed her face eagerly against the window,
but there was little to see. Amid the endless wastes of
red dust Rainbow End looked like a toy town with its
neat white houses and squares of velvety green lawn. As
soon as the plane touched down Rob led the way down
the metal stairs to the tarmac. Impersonally he held out
his hand to help Jo down the final step, but there was no
warmth in his touch.

'We'll get a taxi back to the house,' he said. 'You can
have a look around there, and then I'll drive you down
to the medical centre.'

'All right,' agreed Jo in a subdued voice, brushing
away a couple of flies that were hovering around her
face. 'It's pretty hot, isn't it?'

Rob smiled sardonically.

'This is mild for Rainbow End,' he replied. 'Ninety-five degrees Fahrenheit, thirty five degrees Centigrade. You don't call it hot here until it reaches forty-eight in the shade. But if you don't think you can handle it you can always quit.'

'I can handle it!' flared Jo.

The town was surprisingly pleasant, with wide streets lined with eucalypts and peppercorn trees, and a large, modern shopping centre with shady verandas and a central plaza with a fountain cascading into a rock-pool. But nothing could hide the pervasive red dust. Even the light seemed to have a reddish tinge that turned Jo's hair to a flaming copper halo around her face.

'This is our place, here,' said Rob as the taxi driver drew up outside a white Spanish-style bungalow on a hill overlooking the town. 'I suppose you'd like to see inside.'

Jo shaded her eyes, gazing around as Rob paid off the driver. She had a swift impression of tennis courts, a swimming pool and a garden with big, shady trees.

'I'd rather go down to the medical centre, if you don't mind,' she said. 'After all, I'm sure you'll supply everything necessary for nursing Tom in the house, so I'd really like to see the professional side of things most.'

'Are you sure?'

Rob sounded surprised, but he made no further comment. Opening the double garage, he unlocked a four-wheel-drive jeep, and helped Jo inside.

'Tell me about the practice,' she urged, as he reversed out of the driveway.

'Well, we have three GPs. Myself, Stuart Parker and Amanda Goodridge. Then there's the receptionist, Margaret Buckland, the practice sister Helen Duff, and Pam Morrow, who normally works part-time on the nursing side, but has just gone on maternity leave. The centre is funded by the mining company, and we divide our working time between the mine and the town. My timetable is probably fairly typical. I have ten sessions a week, of which nine are usually Monday to Friday. In a typical week I have one afternoon off and work a half-day on the weekend. Generally I spend three of those sessions at the mine itself and the rest are general practice in the town, looking after the miners' families. I also do regular hospital rounds at eight o'clock every morning before I go to the surgery or the mine. Most of our work is with young families. There are very few old people in a mining town, although a couple of Tom's old cronies do roll up once in a while. Any accident cases are treated at the local hospital if they're not too severe. Otherwise they're stabilised and then flown to Perth.'

'What about Obstetrics?' asked Jo.

Rob's face lit up. 'I'd say I've delivered about half the babies in this town,' he said with pride. 'There aren't many obstetric cases we can't handle here.'

Jo would have liked to pursue the subject, but at that moment they turned a corner and drew up outside a low bungalow style building covered in white stucco.

'Right, here we are, then,' said Rob, parking the car under the shade of a spreading peppercorn tree.

He picked up a white towel and flung it over the steering-wheel.

'What are you doing that for?' asked Jo.

'Keeps the sun off the steering-wheel,' replied Rob. 'It should be OK with the car in the shade, but you never know. You can get quite a nasty burn from the heat in these parts if you forget to cover it.'

He led her into a surgery sheltered from the heat by the inevitable iron lace veranda. As they entered the building the welcome coolness of an efficient air-conditioning system seemed to waft out to meet them. A tall, grey-haired woman in a white uniform paused in the act of covering up a computer.

'Hello, Rob,' she said, smiling. 'You're back early, We didn't expect you till tomorrow.'

Rob smiled, and for an instant the fiend who had been

intimidating Jo all afternoon was transformed into a man of considerable warmth and charm.

'Everything is at sixes and sevens with Tom out of action,' he replied. 'I had some business at the mine to attend to, and I wanted to show Jo the practice. This is Jo Webster. Jo, I'd like you to meet Margaret Buckland.'

The older woman smiled pleasantly at Jo.

'You'll be Pam Morrow's replacement, I suppose?' she said in a friendly voice.

'Not exactly,' cut in Rob brusquely. 'Look, Marg, if you're locking up here don't worry about us. Just go ahead. We'll only be here very briefly, and I guess you want to get away. You've set the answering machine and everything, have you?'

'Yes,' said Margaret with obvious relief. 'Stuart's on call tonight. That's Dr Stuart Parker, Jo. One of our three GPs. Well, if you're sure you don't need me, Rob, I'll be off. Bye, Jo. Perhaps I'll be seeing more of you. . .'

Her voice tailed away uncertainly, but Rob made no attempt to answer any of her unspoken questions. Who is Jo Webster? What is she doing here? Why are you so hostile to her? The moment the door closed Rob began to speak in the flat, measured tones of a tour guide.

'Right. Well, this is the surgery. Here we have the foyer with Margaret's desk, the computer, medical records, switchboard and so on. Over to the side there is a waiting-room and children's play area. Down the corridor here we have three consulting rooms and two treatment rooms. The big one is set up to do small operations, but the other one is pretty basic. The toilets are next to the waiting-room, and the staff tea-room is round the bend in the corridor there. Oh, and we also have a child health clinic attached to the practice. That has a separate entrance from outside, but there's a connecting door next to the tea-room. The mining company pays for the facilities for that, but the State Government funds the nurse. As you can see, it's all a pretty small show. Not the kind of thing you'd be likely to enjoy if you're used to working in large city hospitals.'

Jo looked at him, conscious of a miserable feeling of uncertainty. She wasn't blind or stupid, and she could see perfectly well that Rob Challender didn't want her here. But why? Determined to get an answer, she opened her mouth to ask him, but just at that moment his watch beeped sharply.

'Look, I've got to go,' he said with obvious relief. 'I've got an appointment with the manager of the mine at five-thirty. You can wait for me here if you like, and I'll pick you up later.'

'Couldn't I come?' asked Jo impulsively. 'I've never seen a mine.'

'There won't be much to see. I'm only going to the offices. Oh, all right, then. I can't waste time arguing about it. Come on!'

Half an hour later Jo was sitting outside the mine manager's office, flicking through a magazine and wondering idly why she had ever bothered coming to Rainbow End, when chaos suddenly erupted around her. A siren wailed through the building, and Rob came hurtling out of the manager's office. He grabbed her by the shoulders.

'Do you suffer from claustrophia?' he demanded.

'No. Why? I——'

'Quiet. Listen. There's been an accident down the mine. A bloke was drilling, and he didn't fix the bolts in properly as he went along. Part of the tunnel has caved in on him. They've dug him clear, but he's got suspected spinal injuries. He needs medical attention before they can move him, and he needs it fast. Will you come down with me?'

'Yes, of course.'

'Good girl. Follow me.'

Jo sprinted across the bare ground after Rob. The towering metal headframe above the shaft reared up gold and glittering in the dying sun. As they reached the entrance to the lift a short, stocky man in dirt-stained green overalls strode across to meet them. He shook hands with both of them.

'G'day, Doc. You remember me, don't you? I'm Max Foster, the mine's safety officer. Some of the blokes have already taken our first-aid boxes down below, but is there anything else you need before we go down?'

Rob frowned thoughtfully. 'What do you have in your boxes?' he asked.

'Resuscitation gear, oxygen cylinder, air splints, pain killers, I/V line and drip, all the standard first-aid equipment.'

'Well, that should do for starters,' said Rob. 'Who's the patient, by the way? Anyone I know?'

'Young feller named Ken Lewis. Only bin with us for three months.'

Rob winced. 'Ginger-haired bloke about twenty-five or twenty-six with a wife and two kids?'

'That's the one,' agreed Max.

'What exactly happened to him?' asked Rob.

'The roof of the tunnel fell in,' replied Max. 'He seems to have heard it creaking, and tried to run for cover, but it come down fair on his back. The poor bugger got knocked flat on his face and covered in rocks from the waist down. As a matter of fact, they're still digging him free. He's conscious, but he's pretty crook, Doc.'

'Then we'd better get down to him as fast as we can,' replied Rob. 'He might well have spinal injuries from the sound of things, and it's very important that he shouldn't be moved incorrectly.'

'Yeah, don't worry, Doc. I've drilled that into the men pretty thorough. Come on, I'll get you two some hard hats to wear.'

'Right,' agreed Rob approvingly. 'This is Nurse Jo Webster, by the way. She's coming down the shaft to help me.'

'Good on you, Jo,' said Max. 'Come on, love, and we'll get you kitted out.'

'This could be dangerous, you know,' warned Rob, following Max into the hut next to the shaft and snatching a couple of miners' helmets with headlights from the rack. 'You don't have to come.'

'I know that,' said Jo through her teeth. 'I'm coming anyway.'

Neither of them spoke as they adjusted the headbands, pulled the helmets firmly on to their heads, and stood waiting for the lift to come to the surface. There was a loud metallic clang as a grim-faced miner threw open the yellow metal door of the tiny cage that would carry them two hundred feet below the ground. Jo stepped hesitantly into the lift, followed by the safety officer and Rob, clutching his medical bag.

'Not scared of the dark, are you, love?' asked the miner as he fastened the cage.

'N-no,' said Jo wonderingly.

'Good, 'cause this is the lift we use for the miners, and it doesn't have any lights. The thing is, it goes down so fast the cables would get tangled if we had lights in it. So hold on to your hat.'

Jo's stomach lurched wildly as the lift dropped away beneath them into a pit of darkness. She felt a moment's panic at the thought of the solid walls of rock that encased them, but she clenched her fists and thought of the job in hand. Somewhere down there a man was lying injured and counting on her to remain calm and professional to get him safely out. A sudden flash of brightness outside marked the lift's arrival at the first level of the mine, then they plunged once more into total darkness.

'Nearly there now,' said their guide encouragingly.

The lift shuddered to a halt, and the door clanged open. Ahead of them a tunnel twisted away through the damp, black rocks, lit only by dim electric globes overhead. Dust swirled in the glow from the lights.

'Will we need breathing apparatus?' asked Rob.

'Shouldn't do,' replied Max. 'She's pretty clear now.

There was only the one spot where the roof fell in. It's about two hundred metres away. Come and I'll show you.'

Jo glanced nervously up at the roof as she followed Rob and the safety officer down the tunnel that snaked away into the darkness. It was only about five and a half feet high at best, and in places it came down so low that she had to crouch almost double to get through. But to her relief the timber bearers of salmon gum and black butt looked reassuringly dark and solid in the light from their headlamps.

'There we are,' Max said, turning a corner and gesturing with his thumb.

Jo almost recoiled in horror at the sight in front of her. A plastic box looking incongruously like a telephone booth stood amid the tangled spaghetti of cables leading to half a dozen drills. Its roof was covered with rocks, and only a couple of feet away from it a man lay face down amid a sea of rubble. He was groaning agonisingly while four black-faced miners cautiously levered rocks away from his body. As Jo watched, a small shower of rock fragments fell from the roof on to the victim. Rob glanced up sharply.

'She's as safe as we can make it, Doc,' said Max. 'We've bolted the roof and all. That's how the accident happened—sheer bloody carelessness. Back in the old days you had one miner working one drill, but these days you can put a bloke in a central control box and he can run five or six automatically. I'm always tellin' them, "Every time you drill a hole in the roof, bolt it before you move on to the next one." But some of them get carried away. Poor old Ken here went and drilled six holes in a row before he stopped to put in a roof bolt. He'd just got out to do it, and the whole flamin' lot came down on him. But he's still breathin'. You better see what you can do with him.'

Rob crouched on the damp, gritty floor of the tunnel next to the injured miner.

'How are you mate?' he asked.

The man swore violently and then gave a half-hyster-ical chuckle.

'I've felt better in me time,' he replied curtly.

Jo held her breath as the other miners delicately manoeuvred a huge rock off the patient's lower back. It would be a miracle if he wasn't paralysed, she thought despairingly, after being crushed by such an enormous weight. The man groaned inhumanly as the rock sud-denly came free and was set down on the ground.

'Oh, me back, me back,' he moaned. 'God almighty, Doc, can't you give me something for the pain?'

'Just a minute, mate,' murmured Rob, laying a reassuring hand on his shoulder. 'We need to find out how badly hurt you are first. Now where's the pain?'

'All down me back. No, no, don't touch it!'

Rob looked up swiftly at Max.

'Have you got a spinal stretcher?' he asked.

'Yeah. Up in the office above ground,' he agreed.

'Can you have it brought down then, please?' requested Rob. 'And while we're waiting I think we'd better put in a drip.'

Max gave a swift order to one of the other miners, and then opened one of the safety boxes to find a drip. As soon as he brought it over Jo knelt and spoke reassur-ingly to the patient.

'Ken, I'm just going to hold your arm out here and put the tourniquet on, so that the doctor can get the drip in. Don't worry, we'll have you comfortable just as soon as we can.'

Once she had the drip set up she asked one of the miners to hold the bottle of saline solution, then she steadied the patient's arm as Rob put in the drip. Crouching beside him, she stole a swift glance at his lean, absorbed face as he worked. She was conscious of the immense determination in his blue eyes and intent features. If it were possible to save this man by sheer will-power she felt certain that Rob Challender was the man to do it. His muscular brown arm brushed against hers as the drip went in, and she felt a sudden spark as if a current of electricity had leapt between them. Fighting down an inexplicable sense of exhilaration, she asked the safety officer for some tape, and taped the drip in place.

'Could you check his vital signs now, please, Nurse?' ordered Rob.

'Yes, Doctor.'

There was a short silence as Jo checked the patient's pulse and blood pressure.

'Blood pressure ninety on fifty-four. Pulse a hundred and thirty,' reported Jo.

'Hmm,' said Rob with a sigh. 'Well, I suppose that's only to be expected with a crush injury. But he's probably in a fair bit of pain at that rate. Max, do you carry any strong pain-killers in your box?'

'Yes. But only a doctor can use it.'

'Well, I'm a doctor,' retorted Rob with a touch of impatience. 'What have you got?'

'Morphine.'

'All right. Nurse, can you draw me up——?'

'Ten milligrams of morphine?'

'You read my mind,' said Rob with a swift smile as she handed him the syringe.

Slipping the needle into the arm of the drip, he gave the drug intravenously. Automatically Jo bent forwards and felt the patient's pulse to judge his response to the morphine. The drug was just beginning to take effect when the sound of footsteps in the tunnel announced the arrival of the spinal stretcher.

'Now, this is going to be the tricky bit,' said Rob. 'It's vitally important that we don't do any further damage to Ken's back while we're loading him on to the stretcher, so I'm going to need all your men to help here, Max. Everybody ready? Right, well, I want you all to gather round in a circle and I'm going to put the stretcher down next to Ken. Now I want you all to slip your hands underneath Ken's body and when I say "Go!" I want you all to lift at the same moment. Then, very carefully, keeping his back straight all the time, I want you to turn him over, while I slip the stretcher underneath him. Got it? OK. Go!'

To Jo's relief, the whole operation went smoothly, and soon Ken was safely on the stretcher with rolled-up towels around his body to keep it immobile and a space blanket tucked around him for warmth and a second blanket on top. Jo put another bottle of saline solution in the drip and looked expectantly at Rob.

'Are we ready to go now, Doctor?' she asked.

'Yes, Nurse. Can you manage to hold that bottle up while we carry him along the tunnel? It'll be a bit of a tight squeeze with the stretcher.'

'Don't worry. I'll be careful,' Jo assured him.

'Good. Everybody ready? Then we'll carry him back to the lift.'

On the way up in the lift Jo continued to monitor the patient's vital signs in the pink glow from a fluorescent torch. When they reached the surface she was relieved to find an ambulance standing by with its red light sending pulses of colour across the dark landscape. The ambulance officers came hurrying forward to help with the stretcher.

'Just want him taken to the local hospital, do you, Doc?' asked one of them.

'That's right, Pete, but I'd like you to alert the air ambulance to remain on stand-by. I want to get some X-rays done and get his condition stabilised, but I've a feeling we may need to fly him out to a spinal unit in Perth.'

Ken Lewis's eyes came slowly open. They were glazed with pain and the effects of morphine, but the fear in them went straight to Jo's heart.

'I will walk again, won't I, Doc? Won't I? Won't I?'

Rob smiled sadly. 'Don't borrow trouble, mate,' he advised. 'I'm afraid there's a chance you've broken your back, but wait until we check it out with the X-rays. You could be lucky.'

As the ambulance officers lifted him inside the vehicle the young man gave a hoarse sob and his face crumpled. Swallowing hard, Jo climbed in after him. A moment later Rob joined her. Although he said nothing she was grateful for his warm, silent presence on the journey back to town.

When they reached the district hospital the young miner was soon whisked away for assessment. A plump young woman looking red-eyed and worried was waiting anxiously at the entrance to Casualty as the ambulance came to a halt. She looked no older than eighteen or nineteen, but she had a toddler clinging to one leg and a baby asleep over her shoulder. Jo felt a twinge of sympathy as she saw her pacing restlessly up and down outside the X-ray unit, desperately waiting to hear her husband's fate. An hour and a half later the second batch of X-rays showed both bad news and good news. Unstable fractures of the lumbar one and lumbar two vertebrae. Fortunately, since the young man had been lifted and moved so carefully, there was a good chance that he would make a full recovery and walk again, but he faced at least three months in hospital. Rob sighed as he scanned the X-rays.

'Call Mrs Lewis into the office, would you, please, Nurse?' he asked. 'And you'd better stay with her while I tell her about this. She may go to pieces.'

'What is it?' wailed the girl as Jo summoned her in., 'He's gunna die, isn't he, Doctor? Or be paralysed?'

Rob took her by the shoulders and guided her gently into a chair.

'No, Mrs Lewis,' he said sincerely. 'He's not. In many ways your Ken has been a very lucky man. It's true that he's suffered serious injuries—in fact he's broken his back—but with luck and the right care he should be——'

He got no further.

The girl's fragile self-control snapped, and she let out

a loud, despairing howl, throwing up her hands to cover her face.

'Broken his back!' she screamed. 'Oh, my Gawd! No, no. Not Ken!'

Not surprisingly the baby woke and began to howl in sympathy. His young mother barely seemed to notice, and for an instant it seemed as if the infant and his shawl would both tumble to the floor. Jo stepped forwards but Rob was even faster. With an expertise that astonished her, he rescued the screaming child, wrapped it neatly in the shawl, and passed it across to Jo. Then he resumed his place next to Mrs Lewis. Pulling her hands away from her face, he gazed steadily into her tear-swollen eyes.

'Now, look, Mrs Lewis. Tracey, isn't it?'

She nodded speechlessly.

'Ken is going to be all right. Within six months he'll be walking again just as well as you or I can, except that he may have a slight limp. But he's going to need your help and support to get well, so you mustn't let yourself go to pieces, OK? Especially when you've two lovely kids like this depending on you. Now do you think you can sit down quietly, and Nurse will fetch you a cup of tea while I explain what's going to happen to Ken?'

The girl gave a shame-faced nod. When Jo returned with a cup of heavily sweetened tea Tracey was sitting clasping the baby and hanging on every word Rob spoke.

'So, you see,' he finished, 'Ken will be sent by air ambulance to the regional spinal unit in Perth. He'll have to spend three months flat on his back in a special rotating spinal bed, but after that he'll be able to come home, and within six months he should be as good as new.'

'Truly?' asked the young wife in a tremulous voice.

'Truly,' agreed Rob earnestly.

'Oh, cripes, Doc! I could just kiss you!'

And, with another flurry of the shawl that set the baby howling again, Mrs Lewis did exactly that.

It was after ten o'clock when the air ambulance took off into the starry dark sky above the town.

'Well, it looks as though we'll just have to stay the night at Rainbow End,' said Rob with a sigh. 'The Piper Navajo left hours ago, and there wasn't room for us in the air ambulance.'

'I'm sorry you missed your dinner with Miranda,' said Jo hesitantly.

Rob shrugged.

'Yes, she didn't sound too thrilled when I phoned her,' he admitted. 'Still, one of these days she's just going to have to accept that a doctor's life is like that. Speaking of dinner, are you hungry?'

'Starving,' Jo admitted.

'Well, how does a Chinese take-away sound? And a shower? I feel as if I've been underground in the grit for five years.'

'That sounds great to me,' agreed Jo.

In a companionable spirit they went into Rainbow End's only Chinese restaurant and chose Peking duck, fried rice, honey prawns, steak with black bean sauce and stir-fried vegetables, before driving home to shower and change. Rob produced a stylish red tracksuit for Jo to wear, which she strongly suspected belonged to Miranda Sinclair. However, reflecting wryly that beggars couldn't be choosers, she allowed herself to be sent off to a tiled bathroom, where she sluiced away all the grime from the mine and washed her hair. When she emerged Rob was already in the kitchen, heating the food in the microwave oven and rummaging in the refrigerator for drinks.

'Mmm. That smells good,' said Jo appreciatively.

Rob paused with his hand on the refrigerator door.

'You did well today,' he said curtly.

'Thanks,' replied Jo, surprised to find that his praise sent a current of pure joy tingling right down to her toes.

But then he ruined everything.

'Well, whatever else you may be, you're an excellent nurse,' he admitted gruffly.

Whatever else you may be. Alarm bells rang furiously in Jo's brain. Just what did Rob Challender mean by that? With a challenging toss of her head, Jo put the question she had been longing to ask all day.

'If I'm such a excellent nurse, Dr Challender, then why are you so keen to get rid of me?'

CHAPTER THREE

'Isn't that obvious?' demanded Rob.

Strolling across the kitchen, he set the pitcher full of juice on the table.

'No,' retorted Jo bluntly.

'Oh, come off it,' urged Rob impatiently. 'When we had dinner in Perth you told me that your one big ambition as a nurse was to look after sick kids. You also said that you really couldn't see yourself working anywhere but in a big city hospital. And then good old Tom fronts up, offering twice the award rates for a nurse, and suddenly all Jo Webster's fine principles fly out of the window. So what other reason do you have for taking this job with Tom, apart from lining your pockets?'

His blue eyes were like chips of ice, but Jo matched him stare for stare.

'You don't think that I might just feel sorry for Tom?' she said softly.

'No, I don't, frankly,' declared Rob.

Rage bubbled up deep inside Jo. Down in the mine she had worked as a team with this man, depending on his skills as he had depended on hers. She had begun to feel a deep respect for Rob Challender, and she'd thought she had earned some respect in return. Now it was like a slap in the face to find him insulting her in this way. And Jo was not the kind of person to take that lying down. All right, so he thought she was a gold-digger, did he? Well, let him think it, then! Her eyes narrowed thoughtfully, and she let a cool, superior smile hover around the corners of her lips.

'Well, you're right, of course,' she said airily. 'I am in this only for the money, and Tom is a real old sugar-daddy.'

'What do you mean?' demanded Rob in a hard voice.

'Er——' replied Jo, inventing wildly. 'Well, apart from the wages which are very good, he's already given me the money for a car and a trip to Hawaii. And he's promised me a deposit on a flat when I move back to Perth. Why else would I want to do a job like this?'

'You heartless little schemer!'

Jo flinched as Rob thrust his angry face into hers. He was so close she could see the dark after-five shadow on his chin, the ridiculously long black lashes that fringed his smouldering blue eyes and the grim twist to his lips. For one panic-stricken moment Jo wondered whether she had gone too far as Rob seized her arms and his thumbs pressed fiercely into her tender flesh.

'W-what are you going to do?' she faltered.

'Nothing,' he growled. 'Murder is still a crime in this country. But if you hurt Tom I'll make you wish you'd never been born.'

'You're not going to tell him what I said, then?' whispered Jo.

Of course, Tom might actually appreciate her flight of fantasy, but she couldn't be quite sure of that.

'No,' said Rob through clenched teeth. His grip on her arms slackened, and he thrust her angrily away from him. 'It's Tom's money, after all, and he can spend it however he likes. But you'll be a fool if you take this job, Jo Webster. Because I'll personally guarantee to make your life a misery if you do.'

Jo's chin came up defiantly. She met that intent blue gaze, and for one quivering moment wondered how it would feel if Rob was staring at her like this with passion rather than rage. Then she thrust the thought away.

'Is that right?' she replied coolly. 'Do you know, Dr Challender, I think you've just helped me to make up my mind? I *am* going to take the job.'

With barely controlled savagery, Rob wrenched the lids off the plastic containers and shovelled a turbulent mixture of Chinese food on to Jo's plate. Then he thrust a fork into the centre of the steaming mound and pushed the plate towards her.

'Eat!' he said violently.

It was the last word he spoke to her that evening. They finished the rest of the meal in silence and, when Jo finally rose to wash the dishes, she found them snatched out of her hands and rammed carelessly into the dishwasher. Then Rob strode across to the kitchen door.

'Goodnight,' murmured Jo hesitantly.

He paused long enough to cast her a fierce glare. But his only other response was to slam the door so hard that the casseroles on the shelves rattled nervously.

'Oh, no,' groaned Jo, putting her hands up to her face. 'What have I done?'

She was still wondering about that long after midnight. Her insomnia certainly couldn't be blamed on discomfort of any kind. In fact, the rooms assigned to her were the last word in understated luxury. A spacious sitting-room furnished with chintz-covered settees, carved coffee-tables and blue print curtains led through into a bedroom that would have made any woman utter a sigh of pure pleasure. The room was dominated by a huge bed with an amazing bedhead in the shape of a giant fluted seashell. This was complemented by an elaborate bedroom suite with wardrobes, night tables, chaise longue and stools all carved in ash-blonde wood. The walls were painted a soft apricot shade with accents of blue-grey on the picture rails, and there were blue-grey curtains and carpet to match. The same restful colours were picked up in the luxurious adjoining bathroom. Yet when Jo drew back the crisp blue sheets and climbed into the vast, comfortable bed and snapped off the light she tossed and turned as restlessly as if she were lying on a concrete slab.

Spotting the problem was simple. It was Rob Challender. Yet solving it was another matter. For some reason Rob had taken it firmly into his head that Jo had only helped Tom in order to extract money from the old man, but convincing Rob that her motives were pure wasn't going to be easy. Especially, Jo had to admit, after the pack of lies she had told him tonight. How could she blame him for thinking she was a gold-digger? After all, she was the one who had said she was only after a car, a trip to Hawaii and a deposit on a flat. Jo groaned and pummelled the pillow.

'Oh, my stupid temper!' she wailed aloud. 'Why on earth did I ever say that? And what am I going to do now?'

If she had any sense she would simply fly back to Perth tomorrow and tell Gavin Lyall she didn't want the job. But there were two good reasons for not doing that. In the first place she was becoming genuinely fond of Tom, and she knew how much the old man wanted her to stay. And in the second place she couldn't bear to give Rob Challender the satisfaction of thinking he had scared her away. He might be an excellent doctor— capable, compassionate and reassuring—but he was entirely too big for his boots. Right from the time he had first met Jo he had been rude, overbearing and insulting every single moment that he had spent with her.

No, not every single moment, thought Jo, feeling her cheeks warm in the darkness. There had been that kiss in Mary Lou's front garden. . . Turning restlessly over, she kicked off the sheet and lay stretched out in bed. She pushed her hair off her forehead and a tiny shiver of excitement ran through her as she remembered Rob's touch on her tangled curls, her face, her lips. His kisses had been as deep and intoxicating as a long draught of wine, and it was pure torment to imagine what he might be like if he were actually in bed with her. Another shiver ran through Jo's body, and she rolled on to her side and huddled herself into a defensive ball. Stop that! she told herself savagely. Kissing you was only one more sign of what an unscrupulous brute Rob Challender is. Anyone with half a brain can see that he's head over

heels in love with that awful Miranda Sinclair! No doubt
he'll marry her before long, and she'll make his life a
misery, just the way he deserves.

But for some reason the thought of Miranda Sinclair
marrying Rob and ruining his life made Jo feel unaccountably depressed. This was absurd. If she didn't
calm down soon it would be dawn and she would still be
wide awake. With a deep sigh she switched on the
bedside lamp, climbed out of the bed, and smoothed the
tangled bed covers. Then she walked across to the
dressing-table, picked up the carafe of chilled water that
stood on a tray, and poured herself a drink. Somebody
must have put it there for her, but who? The housekeeper? But hadn't Rob said she left at six o'clock? Rob
himself, then? Impossible! Draining the glass, Jo looked
at herself squarely in the mirror.

'You're going to pieces over this man,' she whispered
to her reflection. 'And it's ridiculous. Absolutely ridiculous. What you have to do is this. Take the job, tell Dr
Lyall you won't accept a cent above the award rates
and, if Rob "Superman" Challender attacks you again,
just brazen it out!'

It was a week later that Tom made the trip to Rainbow
End. One of the company's Piper Navajo aircraft had
been specially fitted out for the journey with a stretcher
and medical equipment, and Jo travelled in the comfortably upholstered aircraft seat next to her patient. In
spite of some breathing difficulties Tom thoroughly
enjoyed the trip, sitting with his face pressed against the
window as much as possible while the red landscape
unfolded like a map beneath them. However, Jo would
have felt much happier without their fellow passenger.
Rob Challender sat in the seat next to the pilot, and
occasionally twisted in his seat to give her a glance full
of antagonism. Yet when they touched down at the
Rainbow End airport she was glad of his help. Although
Tom was fine at ground level, he had needed oxygen

during the flight, and he looked frail and exhausted as Rob propelled him across the tarmac in a wheelchair to a waiting company car. Jo felt his pulse with a worried frown.

'The sooner you're home in bed, the better!' she said firmly. 'And I want you to take it very easy tomorrow.'

Tom might be lying back with closed eyelids and wheezing breath, but his sense of humour was unimpaired.

'Yes, boss!' he whispered mischievously.

But, to Jo's surprise, the old man seemed remarkably bouncy the next morning, and the improvement continued throughout the following week. Yet if nursing Tom was proving extremely easy, living in the Challender household wasn't. Inevitably Jo found herself thrown into situations of considerable intimacy with Rob. In the mornings they often encountered each other in dressing-gowns at the breakfast table or in the briefest of swimsuits in the pool. They shared the morning newspapers and discussed the running of the household together almost as if they were a married couple. In different circumstances it might have been delightful. As it was, it was rather like waiting for the onset of some violent electrical storm. Nevertheless Jo tried her hardest to remain brisk and professional, and keep the welfare of her patient uppermost in her mind.

'Look at this!' she said one night, as Rob came into Tom's bedroom to bid his uncle goodnight. 'That new drug must really be very efficient. His blood pressure's down to a hundred and seventy over a hundred and two. You won't be needing me at all pretty soon if this keeps up, Tom!'

'Good!' exclaimed Tom with spirit. 'That'll suit you, love. Mind you, I like having your lovely cheerful face around the house, but I know you're getting bored with nothin' much to do. Tell you what, Bob. Seein' as how I'm turnin' into such a spring chicken, why don't you take young Jo down to the surgery tomorrow, and keep her busy there?'

Rob's fierce black eyebrows drew together. He seemed to be on the point of refusing, but then a slow smile spread over his face.

'Yes, why not?' he murmured. 'Would you like that, Jo?'

'Y-yes, of course,' stammered Jo. 'Provided you want me, that is.

'Oh, I want you,' Rob assured her in a silky voice. 'I'll enjoy having you where I can keep an eye on you.'

Not only an eye on you, but a boot on your neck, thought Jo sourly the following day. All morning Rob had driven her like a slave overseer, and his failure to detect any sloppy work on her part only seemed to make him fiercer.

'I can't think what's got into Rob,' said Helen Duff, the practice sister, after Rob had snapped at Jo about a missing file which he had mislaid himself. 'I know he's got a hasty temper, but he's not usually so unfair. Perhaps he's had another row with his girlfriend, Miranda.'

'Oh?' murmured Jo in an interested voice, feeling as if her ears were going up on stalks. She had very quickly learnt that in a small town everybody's private life was considered public property.

'I don't know if you've met her,' continued Helen, vigorously swabbing down a trolley with antiseptic. 'But I can't say that Miranda Sinclair is high on my list of favourite people. She's brilliant, of course—one of the top lawyers with the Challender mining company—and well-dressed, and I suppose you could even say she's beautiful, if you like really glamorous *Vogue* model-types. But she always seems to be weighing people up to see if they're smart enough or rich enough or powerful enough to be worth the bother of knowing them. She just isn't very nice, if you know what I mean.'

'I know,' agreed Jo with a sigh. 'I met her in Perth

just after Tom had his heart attack. She really put me down in the sweetest possible way.'

'She would!' commented Helen. 'I can't think what Rob sees in her. I know he's very aloof and a bit of a loner, but he's a terrific bloke and a wonderful GP. But Miranda's only interested in his social status as a doctor, and she's always moaning about how he neglects her for his patients. Personally, I'd be really pleased if some other girl managed to cut her out. Somebody who understands what medical practice is really like.'

At that moment the telephone in the treatment-room buzzed.

'Yes?' said Helen, picking up the receiver. 'Oh, Margaret, no! Not another one? I've just got to go and give an injection to one of Stuart's patients, but I'll ask Jo if she can come.'

She hung up and pulled a face at Jo.

'I'm sorry, Jo,' she said sincerely. 'There's another child with gastroenteritis in the waiting-room, and she's been sick all over the floor, Margaret says. Do you mind going and cleaning up? I'm sorry to ask you.'

'That's all right,' replied Jo, heading for the door. 'Isn't that the fourth one today?'

Helen nodded.

'Yes. It's going to be a real epidemic if this keeps up. Well, at least Rob will be too busy to waste his time picking on you.'

But when Jo arrived at the surgery the following morning Rob called her into his office. He was busy packing sachets of oral rehydration powder into his bag, but he looked up as she hesitated in the doorway.

'Well, don't just stand there,' he ordered. 'Come inside. I'm going to need your help.'

'What for?' asked Jo.

'There's a group of twenty-five or thirty semi-nomadic aborigines camped at Cutler's Springs about an hour's drive out of town. Apparently they've been there for several days, and some of the kids have picked up this

gastroenteritis bug that's going around. I know a lot of
the patients are very shy about coming into the surgery
for treatment, so I'm going out to them. While we're
there, I'll try and do some CDT and Sabin oral immunisations at the same time. You can handle that side of
it for me, if you will.'

'Yes, of course,' agreed Jo.

Twenty minutes later they were skimming along the
road that led north out of Rainbow End. The green
lawns and shady trees of the town had vanished in a
flash and now there was nothing but red earth, tough
grey saltbush, dry gum trees and the vivid blue of the
sky. Not to mention a heat so intense that it seemed to
rise up from the landscape like the blast of a furnace. A
flock of raucous galahs flew shrieking across the road,
dipping and swooping before they came to rest in the
branches of a large tree. Apart from that there was no
sound but the noise of the Land Rover's engine. Rob
drove with his blue eyes fixed as intently on the road as
if they were in a traffic jam on the Sydney Harbour
Bridge and, glancing at that stern profile, Jo felt no
impulse to indulge in small-talk. Then the bitumen came
to an end, and small-talk became an impossibility
anyway. The gravel road was so rough that Jo felt as if
her teeth were being jarred out of her jaws as the Land
Rover jolted over the rough surface, sending up showers
of gravel and choking dust. They had gone about ten
kilometres in this fashion when Jo saw an amazing sight
through the dusty windscreen.

'Look!' she said, shading her eyes and pointing. 'Isn't
that somebody camped out up ahead right in the middle
of nowhere? That can't be the aborigines, surely? There's
only one tent. And what on earth is that old man doing?
He looks as if he's playing the violin to a horse!'

Rob gave a sudden, infectious chuckle, which took Jo
by surprise.

'That'd be right,' agreed, slowing down the vehicle.
'It's Old Clarrie! We'd better stop and say hello to him.

And it's not a horse, by the way, it's a mule. Her name's Clementine, and Clarrie loves her dearly.'

'But who is he?' demanded Jo as the Land Rover bumped to a halt on the dusty verge of the road.

'An old mate of Tom's,' replied Rob with a grin. 'They used to work down the mine at Kalgoorlie together back in the forties before Tom made his big find. He wanted to cut Clarrie in on the profits, but Clarrie wouldn't have a bar of it. Said he wanted to find his own fortune, and he's been looking ever since. He comes out here prospecting with a mule and a pick and shovel, just like they did in the Gold Rush days. He's as mad as a hatter, but a nice old bloke.'

At that moment the old man came ambling towards them with his fiddle and bow still in his hands and Clementine following faithfully behind him. He was a short, wiry-looking man with an enormous, bushy beard the colour of bleached tobacco and a face burnt brick-red by the sun. In spite of the heat he wore ancient moleskin trousers and thick boots as well as a faded blue shirt and a broad-brimmed hat with a fringe of bobbing corks to keep off the flies.

'G'day, Doc!' he said with a grin that displayed a large expanse of pink gums and two or three decidedly hideous teeth. 'Got a new sheila, have you?'

Rob opened the door, and helped Jo out of the vehicle.

'This is Nurse Jo Webster from Sydney,' he murmured formally. 'Jo, this is Clarence Brown.'

'Just plain "Clarrie" will do, love,' insisted Clarrie, tucking his fiddle under his arm and shaking hands vigorously. 'So what brings yez out this way, Bob?'

'We're going out to the aboriginal camp at Cutler's Springs,' replied Rob, brushing a couple of persistent flies off his face and pulling his hat down lower.

'Yeah. I heard some of them kids was a bit crook,' nodded Clarrie sagely. 'Still, you've got time for a cup of tea, haven't you, mate?'

Rob looked doubtfully at his watch.

'Well, I'm not sure——' he began.

'Aw, come on,' urged Clarrie. 'Just a quick one. I've got the billy boiled, and it won't take a minute.'

Rob gave in. 'All right,' he agreed.

Clarrie grinned delightedly.

'Good. I'll make you a bit of tucker too,' he promised. 'I reckon you're both half starved, aren't you?'

The mule gave him an urgent nudge in the back and he pushed her away indulgently.

'No, not you, Clemmie!' he reproved. 'I haven't got no apples left for you, me old darlin', not till we gets back home. She's a wonderful beast, you know. Understands every word you say to her.'

Rob rolled his eyes so humourously behind Clarrie's back that Jo had to choke on a sudden giggle. Pressing her handkerchief to her mouth, she turned back towards the car.

'I'm sorry,' she said indistinctly. 'The flies. . .'

Then an inspriation struck her. Opening the car door, she reached inside and picked up her bag. Rummaging through her lunch-box, she pulled out an apple.

'Perhaps Clemmie would like this,' she suggested.

'Aw, good on yer, love!' cried Clarrie. 'Look, Clemmie! Aren't you a lucky girl? You give the nice nurse a kiss, then.'

To Jo's horror the animal did exactly as she was told. Jo stood completely rigid as the great head butted her in the stomach and the big horsy lips blew warmly against her T-shirt. She caught Rob's gaze and, although he had a perfectly straight face, she saw that he was gasping for breath as if he were in the final throes of bronchial asthma.

'Come on now, Clemmie,' said the old man cheerfully. 'I'll just cut this here apple up for you.'

'It's not funny!' Jo hissed at Rob as they followed the bizarre pair across the uneven red ground to the cleared camp-site. 'I never thought I'd have to be kissed by mules in this job!'

'Wait till you taste Clarrie's tea!' warned Rob. 'Then you'll really have something to compalin about.'

As Clarrie was chopping up the apple on an ancient piece of plank Jo noticed that his right forefinger was red and swollen.

'Have you got a splinter in that finger, Clarrie?' she asked hesitantly. 'Would you like us to take a look at it for you?'

'Yeah, too right. I bin meanin' to get into town and get it fixed up,' admitted Clarrie. 'My shovel split fair in half last week, and a bit of it went into me hand. Didn't seem nothin' worth botherin' about at the time, but it's got real sore these last coupla days.'

Jo went back to the Land Rover and fetched a first-aid kit, a basin and a plastic container of clean water. Seeing Rob eyeing her thoughtfully, she hesitated as she opened the lid of the kit.

'Do you want to do this?' she asked.

'No, I'm sure you can handle it,' he said carelessly. 'Go ahead.'

He watched as she bathed Clarrie's callused old hands in soap and water, dried them and then set to work with tweezers to remove the splinter. When it was finally out, she dusted the finger with some antiseptic powder and wrapped a sticking plaster around it. Then she washed her own hands in a fresh lot of water.

'It looks rather red and sore as if it's infected,' she pointed out. 'Do you want to prescribe an antibiotic for it?'

'There's no point giving him a script,' replied Rob. 'He'll never get it filled. But you could give him a tetanus shot in the arm and an injection of procaine penicillin. One point five grams as an intramusuclar injection in the thigh should do the trick.'

'All right,' said Jo. 'I'll give him half on each side so that it'll be less painful. Clarrie, I'm afraid I'll have to ask you to drop your trousers for me.'

Clarrie gave an outraged splutter.

'Oh, my Gawd!' he protested. And, taking off his ancient hat, he held it coyly in front of the mule's face.

'Don't you look, Clemmie!' he warned.

Once the ordeal was over Clarrie brightened up considerably.

'Now how about a nice cuppa tea?' he suggested.

The tea was every bit as bad as Rob had predicted. As black as tar, stiff with condensed milk, and strongly flavoured with smoke and gum leaves. But the damper, fresh from the ashes of the fire with a hard golden crust and a steaming interior, was delicious, and so were the charcoal-grilled slabs of meat which Clarrie served in tin dishes.

'This meat is wonderful,' said Jo enthusiastically, licking her fingers. 'Is it beef?'

'Nope,' replied Clarrie with satisfaction. 'Camel.'

'*Camel*?' echoed Jo, no longer chewing quite so eagerly.

'Yeah. I shot one of the buggers last month. I reckon there was six hundred pound of meat on him. Put most of it in me freezer back home, but each time I come out on one of these trips I bring a fair-sized slab of it with me. When it starts to go off I know it's time to go home. Nice bit of meat though, ain't it?'

'Mmm. Delicious,' agreed Jo faintly.

'Mind you, it's not near as good as grilled snake. . .' continued Clarrie.

Conscious that Clarrie was warming to his theme and that Jo was looking distinctly queasy, Rob cut in on this promising subject.

'So have you found any gold at all, Clarrie?' he asked heartily.

Clarrie snorted with disgust.

'No, I haven't, mate,' he admitted. 'You know all these years I bin prospectin', and the only gold I've ever took home was GIM.'

'GIM?' asked Jo blankly.

Clarrie gave a wheezy chuckle.

'Gold Illegally Moved. G.I.M. GIM,' he explained.

'Back in the old days at the Hainault Mine at Kalgoorlie
the gold didn't always go into the bosses' pockets, I can
tell you. When me and Tom was workin' down the shaft
we'd often spot a nice bit of gold layin' around lookin'
lonely. Oh, yes, there was a fair bit of GIM took home
one way and another in them days. But I've never found
a damned thing out prospectin' on me own.'

'But you still keep trying?' prompted Rob, with a
glance at Clarrie's old-fashioned tent set up above a
pathetic little windlass and home-made shaft.

'Oh, yeah,' said Clarrie enthusiastically. 'And I'll tell
you another thing. It's there. The gold is there. I can
smell it, like. I know I'm gettin' close to it now, and one
of these days I'm gunna have a big find just like Tom
did, and I reckon I'll be drunk for a week to celebrate.'

Rob rose to his feet and set down his empty tin mug.

'Well, I wish you luck, mate,' he said warmly. 'But Jo
and I will have to be getting along now. So we'll say
goodbye, and leave you to your digging and your
fiddling.'

'All right, mate,' replied Clarrie, wiping his hand on
the seat of his trousers, then shaking hands. 'Goodbye,
Jo. All the best. Now I'll just give the old girl another
little tune before I get back to work. It's her birthday,
yer see, and she likes me to make a fuss of her.'

As they made their way back to the Land Rover they
heard the fiddle shriek protestingly into life and Clarrie's
quavering old voice roaring out 'Oh, My Darling, Oh,
My Darling, Oh, My Darling Clementine'. Jo glanced
over her shoulder, and saw the mule butting the old man
appreciatively in the back. Once inside the vehicle, she
dissolved into helpless giggles.

'I don't believe it!' she cried. 'Wasn't he incredible?'

Rob looked up from stowing the medical kit and the
water container in the back. He chuckled too. 'He's
quite a character,' he agreed. 'And I'm glad you gave
Clemmie the apple. It was very thoughtful of you.'

He sounded faintly surprised, as if thoughtfulness was

the last quality he would have expected from Jo. His blue eyes met hers, and she flushed under their steady scrutiny. It was as if he was trying to penetrate right to the heart of her. As he gazed at her an unwilling smile spread over his face and he actually reached out one hand to her.

'You know, sometimes I think you——' he began.

'Yes?' she responded eagerly.

But he seemed to think better of whatever he was about to say.

'Nothing,' he said flatly. 'Come on. We'd better get moving.'

Rob drove in silence for the next half hour or so, and only when they were nearing Cutler's Springs did he speak again.

'You'll find this morning's session a bit surprising after what you're used to in the city,' he warned. 'Even if you've had a few encounters with urban aborigines you'll find that these people are quite different. In the first place, English isn't really their native tongue. They only speak it as a second language, so there can be severe communication problems. But the really important point is that you must be able to see beyond the superficial things. These people have very few material possessions, and they live in what you might see as squalor. At the very least, the conditions are primitive. But the aborigines are very rich in some of the things that count most. Family relationships, co-operation, concern for one another. I hate to see people patronising them or insulting them.'

'You really admire them, don't you?' said Jo thoughtfully.

'Yes, I do,' admitted Rob, his blue eyes kindling. 'I think we can learn a lot from them if we keep an open mind. And most of them are really nice, friendly, genuine people, but they're inclined to be reserved at first, so I'd like you to take things slowly.'

'Yes, of course,' said Jo.

A moment later they saw a broken-down car, with a stick protruding from the radiator, abandoned on the roadside. Shortly after, the two huge peppercorn trees that marked the entrance to Cutler's Springs came into view. Jo was surprised to find a tin-roofed bungalow crouched next to a muddy yellow waterhole.

'You didn't tell me there was a house here!' she said in surprise. 'Do some of the aborigines live here permanently, then?'

'No,' replied Rob. 'There was a family of white graziers here for twenty years or so, and they built the house. But it was the usual story. They had a few years with good rains, borrowed heavily from the bank, and overstocked the land. Then the rains failed, the cattle began to die, and the bank called in the mortgage. In the end the family went bankrupt and just walked off the land. That was about ten years ago. There's been nobody living here since, although the aborigines often camp right next to the house. There's enough water for them, even though the place won't support a mob of cattle.'

The Land Rover jolted down the rutted dust track and turned a corner. A few yards from the dam Jo saw a camp fire with a group of women sitting in a circle near-by. A couple of blue tarpaulins were stretched in the tree branches overhead, and two or three children lay sleeping in the shade below these. A naked toddler with a runny nose was scuffling through the dust, dragging an old tin on a piece of string. He stopped and stared at them open-mouthed as Rob brought the four-wheel-drive vehicle to a halt under a large peppercorn tree alongside a blue Campervan.

'Looks as though the Crabtrees have beaten us to it!' remarked Rob.

'The Crabtrees?' asked Jo blankly.

'Yes. Bill and Janet are itinerant teachers with the School of the Air, although Janet's on maternity leave at the moment, since she's expecting baby Crabtree

number three next month. They're based in Rainbow
End, but they travel a good bit. Whenever any aborigines on walkabout are in the area Bill always tries to get
out and do some work with the kids. He must have the
big ones shut up in a school-room already, I'd say.
Otherwise they'd all be swarming around the Land
Rover by now.'

But as Jo and Rob climbed out of the vehicle it was as
if a signal had been given inside the house. A swarm of
laughing, shrieking dark children came racing across the
red ground and flung themselves on Rob, begging to be
picked up and swung around. Obligingly he lifted one
squealing boy by his wrist and ankle and sent him
soaring through the air like a sugar glider, then tickled a
little girl in the ribs, and finally swung a toddler up on
to his shoulders before setting out for the house. On the
veranda a group of men were sitting cross-legged,
making intricately decorated boomerangs to sell to the
tourists. Setting the child down, Rob sat casually near
the edge of the group and waited. After a while one of
the men brushed a couple of flies away from his face,
walked across to Rob, and squatted down beside him.

'G'day,' he said. 'You the doctor?'

Rob stretched out his hand with a friendly smile.

'That's right,' confirmed Rob. 'My name's Rob
Challender.'

The man smiled, showing perfect white teeth.

'I'm Jimmy Djapuldjari. My wife Lulu told me you
were comin'. We got some sick fellers here for you to
look at. My boy Johnny and two of the others got the
guts ache bad. You want to see them?'

'Yes, please,' said Rob. 'I'll just set up my things
inside the house so I can take a look at them.'

He turned back and gave Jo an encouraging wave
before disappearing inside the house. Briskly she began
unloading the boxes of equipment from the vehicle, and
looked around at the circle of children who were hanging
back and hiding their faces in each other's shoulders as

they whispered in their own language. But when she called for volunteers to help her carry the boxes of equipment one wide-eyed eleven-year-old stepped bravely forward. To Jo's surprise the child's hair was very blonde and straight, in spite of her dark skin.

'What's your name?' asked Jo, crouching down beside her.

'Joan Japulula,' came the husky reply.

'All right, Joan. Since you're being such a big help to me, would you like one of my jelly snakes?'

Jo produced a sweet from a packet in her bag, and held it up temptingly.

'Me too! Me too!' came the instant clamour. 'I'll help you, missus!'

With the ice broken, Jo made her way up to the house surrounded by an eager escort of children loaded with boxes and plastic bags. Rob was just emerging from the house as they reached the front veranda, and he looked at her in surprise.

'You've been quick!' he marvelled. 'I was just coming back to get all that gear.'

'No need,' said Jo, smiling. 'As you can see, my helpers have it all under control.'

'Just put it in the living-room, kids,' instructed Rob. Then he laid his hand on the arm of an elderly black man with grey, wiry hair, who stood beside him. 'Jo, I'd like you to meet Ken Wunnumurra.'

Ken smiled widely as he took Jo's hand.

'Nice to meet you, missus,' he said in a thick accent. 'The women is down by the waterhole. They be real glad to see you.'

And, with a shy nod, he ambled off to meet some teenage boys who were coming across the dusty yard with rifles and a dead kangaroo slung over their shoulders.

Inside the house it was so dark that Jo could not see clearly for a moment. Then, as her eyes became used to the gloom, she saw that she was in a large bare room with an enormous stone fireplace in the centre of one wall. Some of the wooden skirting boards had been prised off the walls for use as firewood and a battered laminex table and a single chair with the stuffling bulging out lay overturned on the floor. Everything was covered in a thick film of red dust. Jo gave a low sigh of dismay.

'I warned you that it was primitive,' said Rob, looking at her with narrowed blue eyes. 'But if you don't think you can cope with working here I can manage on my own. You can sit under a tree and read or something.'

Jo watched as he swung the table effortlessly upright, gave it a quick wipe with a rag, and set a couple of boxes of equipment on top of it. He was clad only in a thin cotton T-shirt and navy shorts, and his muscles rippled powerfully under the light fabric as he moved. Then he rested his tanned forearms on a box and scrutinised her thoughtfully. His look was wary, but not entirely unfriendly.

'Well?' he prompted. 'Do you want to opt out? I wouldn't really blame you if you do. After all, you were hired to nurse Tom, not to work in a dump like this.'

Jo flushed delicately.

'It's not that!' she protested, looking at him with candid golden eyes. 'I don't mind where I work. I was just thinking how awful it must be for those poor mothers trying to cope with sick kids in these conditions. If I can help them I'll be only too pleased.'

Rob gave her another measuring look, but this time she thought she saw approval in his gaze.

'All right,' he said curtly. 'Then let's go and see how the kids are.'

As they emerged from the house, Bill and Janet Crabtree joined them on the wide veranda outside the front bedroom, which was being used as a school-room. Bill was a tall, thickset man with a mane of gingery-brown hair and a full, russet beard, while his wife was a small, dark-haired woman with dancing brown eyes, clad in a very bulging maternity smock. Rob introduced them to Jo, and then quizzed them about the health of the children in the camp.

'Well, there are two or three of the little ones with diarrhoea,' said Janet. 'Most of them have had no immunisations at all, as far as I can make out, and one little chap has a rather nasty-looking discharge from his ear. So there's plenty to keep you busy.'

'Right,' said Rob briskly. 'We'll go down and talk to the mothers first, and then set to work. We should be able to get everything sorted out in a couple of hours, and then we can head back to Rainbow End.'

Janet grinned.

'Well, don't leave without seeing our puppet show,' she warned, waving one hand, which was covered with a glove puppet in the shape of an appealing, furry possum. 'It's going to be the highlight of the Cutler's Springs entertainment season. Starring Charlie Wunnamurra as the Giant Devil Dingo and Janet Crabtree as the Thieving Possum, chief set designer and noises off.'

Rob laughed. 'We wouldn't miss it for the world,' he vowed. 'Now, come on, Jo, we've got work to do.'

He led Jo across to the group of aboriginal women who were sitting in a circle near the camp-fire close to the waterhole. They were all barefoot, dressed in old cotton skirts and dusty T-shirts with pictures of the Muppets on the front, but they smiled warmly as Rob squatted down beside them and introduced Jo.

'Hello,' he said. 'This is my nurse, Jo Webster. Jo, I'd like you to meet Maisie Japulula, Lulu Djapaldjari, Mary Wunnumurra and Patsy Japulula. I hear you got some sick fellers here, eh?'

'That's right,' confirmed one of the women who was suckling a child who appeared to be two or three years old. 'They got the guts ache bad, Doctor. You take a look at my Johnny.'

She made a barely visible movement with one hand,

and a child who was playing on the far side of the
waterhole scuffed shyly through the dust to join them.

For the next couple of hours Jo and Rob were fully
occupied. Three of the younger children had gastroenteritis, and Rob had to explain to their worried mothers
how the oral rehydration programme worked. He
handed out sachets of Repalyte, and held up a large
lemonade bottle to show how much fluid each child
should drink before bedtime. Then, when some of the
adults had been checked for respiratory ailments, they
set to work to do the immunisations. There were nine
children in the group, and none had had a full quota of
the routine immunisations that most city children would
get. When Rob had done a quick general examination
on all the children Janet Crabtree helped to marshal
them into a line, and they went to work. Jo had no
trouble getting the youngsters to accept their Sabin oral
vaccine against poliomyelitis. The pink, sticky syrup
went down like magic, and a couple of die-hard seven-
year-old boys even begged for seconds. But the injections
to protect them against tetanus and diphtheria were
another matter. After a couple of the older children had
been jabbed in the arm and burst into loud yells of
protest panic set in and the remaining six broke ranks
and fled. An energetic chase ensued until the last
squealing five-year-old was dragged from under the
house and vaccinated.

'Phew!' said Rob. 'It's worse than chasing calves. Now
all I've got to do is syringe young Charlie's ears, and we
can all come and watch your puppet show, Janet. But I
think we'd better use the sitting-room as a surgery
instead of the veranda this time. I don't want any more
escapees.'

Jo had done her best to clean out the school-room,
and there was a strong smell of disinfectant in the air,
but nothing could improve the ruined lathe and plaster
of the walls, or the broken window panes that let in the
dust and flies. Still, thought Jo, they would just have to

make the best of the conditions they had. Fortunately
Rob had packed some sterile sheets in the Land Rover,
and she threw one of these over the battered table and
set out the instruments carefully. An aural syringe with
a removable nozzle, a head mirror, a battery-operated
fluorescent lamp, saline solution for syringing, a lotion
thermometer, aural forceps, dissecting forceps, fine wool
swabs, a kidney-shaped receiver for the returned lotion,
a paper bag for soiled swabs, and a receiver for soiled
instruments.

'Ready?' she asked the little boy with a friendly smile.

His dark eyes widened apprehensively, but he nodded.
Briskly she hoisted him into place, and spread another
sheet over his clothes to protect them.

'Ready now, Doctor,' she said.

'Good,' replied Rob, glancing approvingly at the array
of instruments. 'Have you ever done this procedure
yourself, Nurse?'

Jo shook her head.

'Well, it's something you probably ought to learn,'
advised Rob. 'Especially if you're ever going to work
with Outback kids again. Ear infections and obstructions
are a big problem out here. The main danger is that an
unskilled person could easily perforate the eardrum. It's
also very important to have the temperature of the lotion
right at body temperature. If it's above or below the
patient could suffer giddiness, or faint. Now would you
like to just check the temperature of the lotion for me?'

There was a pause while Jo put the thermometer in
the jug and waited.

'Thirty-eight degrees,' she said.

'Good. Now just get Charlie to hold the stainless steel
receiver up against his cheek under his ear, and we'll get
to work.'

Rob put on the head mirror, and arranged the lamp
so that the light would be reflected in the mirror. Then,
after washing and drying his hands, he attached the
nozzle to the syringe.

'Now the syringe is filled and the air has been expelled,' he explained. 'So with one hand I draw the pinna upwards and slightly backwards to straighten the external meatus, then with the other hand I hold the syringe and direct the lotion first along the roof of the canal and then along its floor. That's it!'

When the irrigation was finished, Rob gently dried the ear using dressed aural forceps, and dropped the used material into the paper bag. Then he inspected the ear for any damage or infection.

'Clean as a whistle,' he announced with satisfaction. 'There you go, Charlie. You should hear a lot better now. So off you go to the barn for the puppet show. And tell them not to start until we get there.'

'OK, mate!' cried the little boy joyfully, and he shot out the door like a rocket.

Ten minutes later Rob and Jo had just finished cleaning up and were coming out on to the veranda when they saw Charlie hurtling back towards them. But he was no longer smiling.

'What is it, Charlie?' demanded Rob as the boy skidded to a halt. 'What's happened?'

'Mr Crabtree say you gotta come right now, Doctor!' Missus Crabtree, she bin hurt real bad. She bleed everywhere!'

CHAPTER FOUR

HORRIFIED, Jo and Rob raced towards the bar. But when they reached it they realised that Charlie had spoken no more than the simple truth. Janet was lying on the floor in a pool of blood next to an overturned step-ladder surrounded by a ring of anxious, jabbering children. Her husband Bill was kneeling beside her, and gazed up with a white, terrified face as he heard them enter the barn.

'What happened?' demanded Rob, his gaze flying to the overturned ladder. 'She didn't fall off that, did she?'

'Hmm,' whimpered Janet. 'Sorry... Such a stupid thing to do... Bill had gone out to the van to get something...wanted to hang the curtains... Feel such a fool——'

She gave a sudden gasp as if a spasm of pain had caught her unawares, and clutched suddenly at her abdomen.

'Well, it's done now,' said Rob sharply. 'There's no point blaming yourself. What we've got to do is see how badly hurt you are. Bill, get these kids out of here, and then use my car radio to call the flying doctor service at Kalgoorlie. Explain what's happened, and ask them to stand by in case we need them. Jo, go and get me some more clean sheets from the Land Rover and my medical bag from the school-room.'

When Jo came racing back Rob helped her to slip the clean sheet under the injured woman so that he could examine her. But even as his deft, gentle fingers were probing Janet's abdomen the woman gave another gasp and clenched her fists. Instinctively Jo looked at her watch and began to count. Rob gave a worried sigh.

'Just as I feared,' he said. 'It's an abruptio placentae

and it looks as though the shock of the fall has brought on her labour. What's the length of the contraction, Nurse?'

Jo waited until Janet let out her breath in a long sigh.

'Forty-six seconds,' she replied.

'And the first one was. . .how long ago?'

'Four minutes.'

'Right. We'll need the flying doctor for sure. Run down and tell Bill to get back to them on the radio and tell them we want them as fast as they can get here. Tell them it's an abruptio placentae with moderately severe bleeding. She's going to need a blood transfusion as soon as possible. Janet, do you know what your blood type is?'

'O Positive,' said Janet weakly. Tears squeezed out under her eyelids. 'Rob, I'm not going to lose my baby, am I?'

Rob squeezed her hand reassuringly, and mouthed the word 'Hurry!' to Jo. 'We'll do all we can to save him,' he promised.

For the next half-hour Rob and Jo were fully occupied trying to keep that promise. They had just finished setting up a drip when Bill came back from the Land Rover looking haggard and anxious.

'How is she?' he asked urgently, looking down at Janet's white, contorted face.

Rob gave him a swift, measuring look.

'She's suffering from an abruptio placentae,' he explained. 'What that means is that the placenta is separating from the wall of the uterus and that's what's causing the bleeding. The fall has also brought on contractions, and she's in the early stages of labour.'

'Oh, hell!' groaned Bill.

'Now, look, mate,' said Rob. 'She's thirty-seven weeks' pregnant and it's a good-sized baby. If she had a separation of the placenta like this and she was in hospital I'd have to bring on labour anyway to try and save the baby. Except that in hospital I'd be able to give her a blood transfusion. But with luck the flying doctor service will get a plane out here soon, and they'll both be fine. If she doesn't lose too much more blood everything should be OK.'

'And if she does?' demanded Bill desperately.

'We'll cross that bridge when we come to it,' replied Rob curtly.

Bill pounded his fist into the palm of his other hand.

'I wish there was bloody something I could do!' he exclaimed in frustration.

'There is,' said Rob. 'This barn is filthy, and I don't want to take a chance of Janet giving birth in here, so I want to move her. How's the inside of your camper van? Pretty clean?'

'Yeah, you could eat off the floor,' confirmed Bill with a worried glance at his wife. 'Jan scrubbed it out just before we left home yesterday.'

'Good,' replied Rob. 'Well, we'll put her in there. And after that you can go out and make sure the airstrip is clear for the plane to land.'

Once they had moved Janet into the camper van events went steadily from bad to worse. It was now fifteen minutes since she had fallen from the ladder, and he labour was strongly established and progressing fast. But unfortunately she was still continuing to haemorrhage quite severely, and all Rob's efforts could not stem the loss of blood. Accustomed to life in the Outback, he never travelled far without a fairly comprehensive medical kit, but he was not equipped to do a blood transfusion. The best he could do was to set up a saline drip, and pray for the swift arrival of the plane. As the minutes dragged by Jo monitored the patient's vital signs and felt a sinking sensation in the pit of her stomach. Janet was coping gallantly with the fierce contractions that were gripping her body, but the loss of blood was beginning to tell on her strength.

'Vital signs, Nurse?' demanded Rob, his stethoscope

pressed against Janet's swollen abdomen, and his face grave.

'Pulse one hundred and thirty-two. Blood pressure a hundred over sixty.'

Jo heard his swift, ragged intake of breath.

'Damn! The foetal heartbeat has dropped to ninety, which means we're in severe trouble. She's got to deliver soon!'

At that moment Janet, who had been amazingly quiet and co-operative up to this point, suddenly pushed aside Rob's stethoscope with a petulant movement and sat up.

'You're both completely useless!' she cried in a voice edged with hysteria. 'Why don't you do something to save my baby? I hate you, both of you!'

Then she promptly burst into tears.

Jo immediately recognised this emotional storm for what it was.

'She's in transition!' she said firmly. 'She'll be in second stage any moment now.'

'I think you're right,' agreed Rob jubilantly. 'Well, that means we're in with a chance. Come on, Janet! Don't give up now, you've got to get this baby born!'

Janet's only response was to clench her teeth and give a long, despairing groan.

'There she goes!' applauded Jo. 'Come on, Jan! A big breath and then push!'

'I want to sit up,' gabbled Janet.

'All right,' agreed Rob. 'We'll help you.'

Together they put their arms under Janet's shoulders and helped her into a squatting position. As they did so Jo heard the unmistakable drone of an aeroplane engine coming closer. She caught Rob's eye and saw the wild flare of hope that passed over his face. Then Janet's body went into another spasm of pain and effort and they were both too busy to do anything but work. It was stiflingly hot in the camper van, and all three of them were drenched with sweat, but Janet was also becoming alarmingly pale from loss of blood.

'I feel giddy,' she complained.

'Never mind!' coaxed Rob. 'Come on, Jan. One more push. You can do it!'

Janet gave a feeble moan, and they felt her slight body strain under their hands. Then there was a sudden gush of fluid and the baby shot out wet and slippery on to the bed. He was bluish-grey in colour and not breathing, but Rob hastily cut the cord and picked up the tiny, motionless body.

'Deliver the placenta,' he instructed hastily.

Then he went to work to try and revive the infant with mouth to mouth resuscitation. There was no response. Swearing softly, Rob applied external cardiac massage in a desperate attempt to get the child's heart beating. Meanwhile Jo was fully occupied with Janet. Although the patient had succeeded in expelling the placenta the effort seemed to have exhausted all her remaining strength. She lay with her eyes closed and her face sweating and ashen-pale, her breath coming in fast, shallow gasps. But at that moment there was the sound of running feet outside the van as the Royal Flying Doctor team arrived.

Rob uttered a few, curt instructions, and Jo found herself hastily ushered outside the van so that the second doctor could take her place. For the first time since the drama began she had the leisure to look around her. Twenty paces away she saw Bill Crabtree standing under one of the peppercorn trees looking as if he had been turned to stone. His eyes were closed and his hands were clenched into a rigid spire as if he were praying. The pitiless sun beat down on the red earth just as fiercely as before, but there was none of the gaiety that had marked the little encampment when Jo first arrived. The aboriginal children huddled in a silent, anxious throng on the shady veranda, and even the women had stopped talking.

It seemed like hours that Jo stood there, leaning against the dusty red surface of the van with the hot

breeze fanning her cheeks, but it could not have been
more than ten minutes. At last there was a grinding
rattle as the side door of the van opened and Rob
stepped out. Jo started forward, but one look at his face
told her all she needed to know. Slowly and gravely he
shook his head. Then he walked across the twenty paces
of open ground to where Bill stood under the peppercorn
tree. Bill's eyes flew open.

'Janet?' he whispered hoarsely.

'She's going to be all right,' said Rob heavily. 'But
I'm afraid we weren't able to save the baby.'

Bill gave a strangled groan, and Rob put his arm
around the other man's shoulders. Slowly the two men
walked around the edge of the waterhole, deep in
conversation. Jo's eyes blurred with tears as she saw
them go.

She was still crying ten minutes later when the plane
took off, bearing the Crabtrees back to Rainbow End.
Then a shadow fell across the ground in front of her.
Turning hastily, she saw Rob's sombre blue eyes gazing
down at her.

'I suppose we'd better go,' he said in a subdued voice.

She nodded, not trusting herself to say anything. His
hand came out and touched her cheek.

'Tears?' he asked softly.

'I can't help it,' she choked.

His hand came down on to the nape of her neck and
moved soothingly down over her sun-warmed flesh,
kneading away the tension in her muscles. She was so
close to him now that she could feel the steady beating
of his heart as well as the almost absent-minded caress
of his fingers. For a moment she felt a blind, overpowering urge to burrow into those powerful arms and beg
him to hold her. Then she took a deep breath and
regained control of herself.

'Do you want me to drive Bill's van back to town for
him?' she asked.

'No, that won't be necessary. One of the aboriginal

men has offered. Apparently he wants to go into town anyway.

Jo let out her breath in a ragged sigh.

'Good,' she said frankly. 'I was dreading the task, but I thought I should at least offer.

They were both silent as they packed up their equipment and prepared to leave. After a swift farewell to the aboriginal families they were soon in the Land Rover and back out on the rutted, country roads. For a long time the noise of flying gravel made conversation impossible, and in any case neither of them felt like talking. But Jo could see from the tempestuous look on Rob's face that his thoughts were anything but calm.

'Do you want to talk about it?' she asked hesitantly when they hit the smoother surface of the bitumen road.

'About what?' asked Rob harshly, ramming the vehicle into a higher gear and gathering speed. 'About what a rotten doctor I am?'

'Oh, Rob, don't be ridiculous! It wasn't your fault!'

'Wasn't it?' he retorted. 'Well, it always feels like it. You know, I love Obstetrics. Usually everything goes well and, however many babies I deliver, the whole thing always seems totally miraculous to me. And yet when something like this happens I'm devastated. Utterly devastated. So much so that I wonder why in hell I ever wanted to be a doctor, or why I ever thought I was any good at it. Maybe if I'd done something different I could have saved that baby today.'

'No, you couldn't,' said Jo with conviction. 'You did everything possible. You shouldn't blame yourself for it. Besides, it was touch and go for Janet too. If you hadn't been there she could easily have bled to death.'

Rob was silent, staring grimly down the dusty road, his face screwed into a ferocious glare. For all the response he gave he might just as well not have heard Jo's words. Her own fragile patience snapped, and she flared up at him.

'Oh, stop being so bloody-minded about it!' she

exclaimed. 'You know perfectly well that you saved Janet's life out there today. And it wasn't your fault the baby died, so stop being melodramatic about it! Anyway, if you want to know the truth, I feel pretty badly about it, too. I'm starting to think I should have been anything in the world rather than a nurse!'

Tears suddenly overtook her again, and she stared out at the harsh, red landscape, swallowing hard as she fought for control.

'Oh, come on,' urged Rob in a voice full of concern. 'You're not blaming yourself too, are you?'

'Of course I'm blaming myself!' snapped Jo.

The tears squeezed out under her eyelids and rolled down her cheeks. She had to clamp her mouth firmly shut to stop her chin from quivering. After a couple of deep breaths she went on.

'If you really want to know,' she admitted unsteadily, 'I always feel this when a child dies. Even if it's something like leukaemia or massive road trauma— something where I couldn't possible have prevented it. I know you're supposed to stay detached but I just can't. It's like a deep, black hole that I fall into. Every single time. But somehow you just climb out of it and keep going. You have to.'

There was a long pause.

'I know,' replied Rob at last. 'You're right, of course. Anyway, just for the record I think you're a damned good nurse! One of the best I ever worked with. Calm, professional, quick-thinking, compassionate. . .'

Jo gave a watery smile.

'Not to mention rude and outspoken,' she added.

'That too,' agreed Rob with a sudden wry grin.

'Well, I think you're a damned good doctor,' rejoined Jo sincerely. 'One of the best *I* ever worked with.'

Rob's lean brown hand came off the steering-wheel and rested fleetingly on Jo's wrist. Her heart gave a tumultuous leap as if some current of warmth had passed between them.

'Thanks,' he said.

Then he turned his attention back to the road.

When they reached Rainbow End it was after five
o'clock. The surgery was already locked up with the
outside light beginning to glow yellow against the gathering dusk. Jo was frankly relieved. After the stresses of
the day she didn't feel like talking to anyone, even
another health worker.

'What do you want to do now?' asked Rob, as he
backed the Land Rover into the car park. 'I've got to
take my gear inside, and I want to ring the hospital to
check on how Janet's getting along, but if you need a lift
anywhere after that I'll be glad to take you. You did
mention yesterday that you were thinking of playing
tennis with Margaret Buckland tonight.'

Jo pulled a face.

'I know,' she said with a sigh. 'But I don't think I can
face it tonight. I'll just ring and cancel. All I want to do
now is put these instruments in the steriliser, take a
shower, and have a long, quiet evening without having
to talk to anyone.'

'I know how you feel,' agreed Rob sympathetically.
'The last thing I could face tonight would be a big group
of people. So let's just go home, have a swim, barbecue
some steaks, and just wind down. How does that sound?'

Jo looked at his lean, suntanned face, the dazzling
blue eyes and the wind-tossed black hair. A sudden
tremor of nervousness or excitement pulsed through her,
which was strange. After all, it was not as though Rob
was proposing anything very extraordinary. It was just
the kind of evening a husband and wife might spend
together after a long and harrowing day. But perhaps
that's it, she thought slowly. Perhaps that's what I really
want from him. She looked back into those intent blue
eyes, which were no longer cold and hostile, but warm
and almost affectionate. And, with a sudden stab of

certainty that pierced her right to the heart, she knew that she wanted to marry Rob Challender.

'Well?' he quizzed.

'Yes,' she said huskily. 'Yes, please.'

While Jo was sterilising the instruments they had used at Cutler's Springs Rob phoned through to the hospital. As soon as she'd finished switching on the steriliser, labelling the dirty laundry bag and stowing away the rest of their equipment Jo tiptoed along the corridor to Rob's consulting-room. He saw her hovering outside the open door, and motioned her inside.

'All right, mate,' he said into the receiver. 'I'll talk to you again tomorrow, Goodbye.'

'Well?' demanded Jo.

A faint smile touched the corners of his mouth and crinkled his eyes.

'Good news,' he said with relief. 'Janet's out of danger. Apparently she's very upset about the baby, but that's only to be expected. They say she's sleeping now, and they expect her to be out of hospital by the end of the week.'

Jo let out her breath in a long sigh.

'That's good,' she said softly. 'Poor thing, she'll have a hard time for the next few weeks, though. I must pop in and see her in a couple of days.'

'Yes, do that,' advised Rob. 'She'd probably appreciate it. So what now? Shall I take you home?'

Jo looked down at her soiled white uniform and shuddered.

'Do you mind if I take a quick shower and change here first?' she asked. 'I can't possibly go into Tom's nice, clean house looking like this. All I want to do is strip off and really give myself a thorough soaking.'

'Good idea,' replied Rob. 'In fact, I think I'll join you.'

Jo's tawny eyes widened in alarm and Rob gave a throaty chuckle of amusement.

'Well, not exactly join you,' he amended. 'Imitate you is what I meant. But you go first.'

Before long Jo was standing under the warm torrent of the shower, twisting lithely about as she shampooed her long tawny-brown curls. Raising her arms caused her full, white breasts to tilt provocatively, and she looked down at her own body with a sense of mingled excitement and misgiving. What would it be like to have Rob in the shower here with her? To see that powerful masculine frame stripped in all its rugged glory? She had seen him several times in the swimming pool at Tom's place, churning up and down in the cobalt-blue water, and then hauling himself out with the muscles in his suntanned arms standing out like tense whipcords and his deep chest sleek with wet, dark hair. But what would it feel like to have him standing here thigh to thigh with her, while those lean brown hands caressed her creamy-white flesh? Would he find her attractive? she wondered uncertainly. Jo was generously built, definitely more of an Amazon than a slender, elegant model. Could she ever compare with a woman like Miranda Sinclair? Somebody elegant, sophisticated, brilliant? And, even if Rob ever did find her attractive, wouldn't he simply throw her over in the end for somebody more glamorous? Just the way Bruce Fielding had?

Jo gave her hair a final vicious twist to squeeze out the last of the shampoo, ducked back under the full onslaught of the shower to rinse it, and then turned off the tap. It was a long time since she had thought of Bruce Fielding, although as a junior surgeon at Royal North Shore he had occupied her thoughts almost day and night for two years. It was an intensely emotional affair, at least on Jo's part, and somehow she had always expected that when Bruce's career was more firmly established marriage would follow. Which had made it all the more of a blow when Bruce had suddenly headed off for Europe with a Sydney socialite he had met on holiday in Singapore, leaving Jo with nothing but bitter memories. At the time she had found it heartbreaking, but now, three years later, she was forced to admit that hearts were not quite so easily broken as she thought.

Towelling herself briskly, Jo picked up her towel and wiped a little window in the steam on the mirror. For some reason her spirits were beginning to rise and, as she surveyed her freckled nose, her tawny eyes and her wide, generous mouth, she smiled slightly.

'Perhaps Bruce did me a favour,' she murmured softly to her reflection. 'I'd never have met Rob Challender if I had married Bruce, and I'm beginning to think Rob was well worth meeting.'

When she came out of the bathroom Rob was waiting outside with an armful of clean clothes. She blushed hotly, wondering whether he had overheard her foolish comments. But he simply gave her a brief, abstracted smile, and strode into the bathroom. And, from the brooding expression on his face, she knew that he was thinking about the lost baby again.

Night fell swiftly at Rainbow End, and it was already dark when they turned into the tree-lined crescent where Tom's house was situated. To Jo's surprise they were met by a blast of loud music from a full-scale brass band.

'What the hell is going on here?' demanded Rob irritably, turning into the brick-paved driveway of the house, and coming to a halt in front of the elaborate wrought-iron gates. 'Who on earth are these people?'

Jo was still staring in astonishment at the figures in cocktail dresses and evening suits, who were milling around inside the gates, when suddenly a tall, glamorous woman in a red silk trouser-suit detached herself from the crowd and came towards them. Rob climbed out of the Land Rover and stood with his arms folded, glaring suspiciously as she came out of the shadows into the circle of light near the gates.

'Darling!' cried Miranda joyfully, wrenching the side gate open, and staggering in her high-heeled sandals. 'Oops, silly me! You're just in time.'

'Just in time for what?' demanded Rob grimly.

'Well, the surprise party, of course,' said Miranda, taking a quick sip from the long, slender champagne-glass in her right hand. 'Just a little cocktail party I organised to celebrate the thirty-fifth anniversary of the day Tom found the Laurel Wreath nugget at Rainbow End. Today's the fifteenth of April, or had you forgotten?'

'Yes, I had,' retorted Rob tersely. 'Tom's never made a fuss about it before, and nobody told me there was a party planned.'

'Well, of course not!' exclaimed Miranda, pouting provocatively. 'There wouldn't have been any surprise, then, would there?'

'No, there wouldn't,' said Rob through his teeth. 'Because there wouldn't have been any party if I'd known about it. Tom's far too sick for this sort of caper.'

'Oh, darling, don't be such a bore!' protested Miranda. 'Tom's out there by the pool having the time of his life. And so should you be. But just slip in the side door and change out of those dreadful clothes first, won't you?'

Her gaze slid disparagingly down over Rob's denim jacket, striped T-shirt and blue jeans. Then, for the first time, she seemed to notice Jo standing beside him.

'You might like to join us too,' she said sweetly. 'Geraldine, isn't it? Then you can keep an eye on Tom, so Rob can dance with a clear conscience. There's no need for you to change, of course. Tom won't care what you look like, and nobody else is likely to notice, are they?'

Jo stared stonily back at her. Arsenic is too good for this woman, she thought furiously. But before she could say anything Rob stepped into the breach.

'Don't talk to Jo as if she's some third-rate skivvy, Miranda,' he said coolly. 'And thanks for the invitation, but I'm in no mood for dancing tonight. So if you'll just step aside I'll check that Tom really does want this damned fool party on here. And after that I'm leaving.'

'But you can't!' protested Miranda. 'Everybody who's anybody is here. I've had a whole planeload of people brought up from Perth, and Stephen Lester has a Channel One television crew in a van up the road, just waiting to come down and film the whole thing the minute I give the word. It'll be the TV scoop of the decade, and I want you to be in it with me.'

Rob was staring at her, aghast.

'Did you say television crew?' he demanded. 'Have you gone out of your mind, Miranda? Don't you know how much Tom hates publicity and the media?'

'I know he says he does,' retorted Miranda, looking down at her own long, red fingernails curved possessively around the glass. 'But that's a lot of nonsense. If this company is going to go forward into the nineties and retain its competitive edge, then, as I see it, a lot of things are going to have to change. And that includes this ridiculous refusal of Tom's to make personal appearances in the media. In my opinion Tom's perfectly fit to do it. It's just that he chooses not to.'

'Perfectly fit to do what?' asked a suspicious voice at Miranda's elbow.

Jo craned her neck and saw the old man shuffle slowly out the gate to join Miranda, with a glass clutched in one wrinkled brown hand.

'Hello, Tom,' she said with relief. 'How are you feeling? Did you remember to take your tablets at four o'clock?'

'I'm as fit as a fiddle,' declared Tom stoutly. 'I took me tablets, and young Stuart Parker from the surgery come down only an hour ago and checked me blood pressure. He reckons I'll be running marathons any day now, so don't you worry about me, love. But what does Miranda want me to do?'

'A television interview with Stephen Lester,' replied Rob with a furious glance at Miranda.

Tom raised one knobbly, arthritic finger and held it
up to Miranda's face.

'Now listen here, my girl,' he said fiercely. 'That's
goin' too far. I don't mind a bit of a knees-up and a
drink with me friends, but I've never given interviews in
me life, and I'm not about to start now. So you tell your
mate Stephen that he's welcome to come in and have a
drink with me, but if he brings a cameraman along I'll
throw the bugger in the swimmin' pool and his camera
after him. Have you got that?'

Miranda's cheeks burned, but she knew when she was
beaten.

'Yes, Tom,' she muttered.

'Good,' said Tom. 'Well, that's settled, then. Are you
two comin' in for a drink with me?'

Rob cast a swift glance at Jo, and she felt her heart
sink. The last thing she wanted to do was go and
celebrate with a group of noisy, riotous people she had
never even met before. But to her relief she saw the same
reluctance mirrored in Rob's face.

'No, thanks, Tom,' he replied regretfully. 'I don't
think either of us could face it tonight, if you don't
mind.'

Tom nodded, unperturbed.

'Well, you know your own business best, mate,' he
agreed. 'I won't push yez, if you've had a hard day. But
I reckon I'd better be gettin' back to the party.'

With a nod to Rob and an encouraging wink to Jo, he
walked slowly away. He was barely out of earshot before
Miranda launched into a furious outburst.

'Honestly, Rob!' she exclaimed. 'Sometimes you just
make my blood boil. Why on earth did you have to
spring it on him about the TV interview like that? I'm
sure he would have said yes, if I'd only had a chance to
present it to him the right way.'

'Oh, no he wouldn't,' murmured Rob with an undertone of amusement. 'You don't know Tom very well if

you believe that, Miranda. He's as stubborn as they come.'

'Like you!' flared Miranda, tapping one toe angrily on the paving stones. 'Hard day, my eye! Sticking needles into five-year-olds. What's so hard about that?'

'We had a medical emergency,' snapped Rob. 'A baby died.'

'Oh,' said Miranda, taken aback for a moment. Then swiftly she recovered herself. 'Well, what if it did? That's part of your job to cope with that, isn't it? It can't be the first time it's happened, surely?'

'No,' ground out Rob. 'It isn't the first time and it won't be the last time, but however many bloody times it happens it's still painful and hard to deal with. But I wouldn't expect you to understand that. You're so damned cold and clinical, a computer looks positively cosy compared to you.'

Miranda gave a faint, cat-like smile as if Rob had paid her a compliment.

'Well, if you can't take the heat, darling, why don't you stay out of the kitchen?' she purred.

'And what the hell is that supposed to mean?' demanded Rob.

'You know perfectly well what it's supposed to mean,' retorted Miranda. 'Give up this ridiculous idea of being a country GP and move back to Perth into a job that really suits you.'

'You mean get a post in obstetrics in Perth?' asked Rob warily, but with a hint of interest.

'No, I don't mean get a post in obstetrics!' flared Miranda. 'I mean chuck in medicine altogether and take on the job Tom always wanted you to do. A couple of years as an executive and then chairman of the Board at Challender's.

Rob gave a hoarse, disbelieving laugh.

'Miranda, we've been over and over this!' he exclaimed. 'You know damned well I don't want a job as a mining executive!'

'Well, if you can't handle the job you've already got, what other choice is there?' taunted Miranda. 'Why don't you simply throw yourself over the edge of the Super Pit in despair?'

Rob looked at her for a full minute, his blue eyes blazing in the tense lines of his face. Then, in a voice soft with rage, he finally replied.

'I might just do that!' he said.

Then, turning on his heel, he strode off down the dark, tree-lined street. For an instant Jo and Miranda stared at each other in mutual dislike. How could she? thought Jo, appalled. She's supposed to love him. Surely she'll go after him, and explain that she didn't mean it? But Miranda did nothing of the kind. With a low cry of exasperation she turned and marched back through the open gateway to the party.

Left alone, Jo gazed anxiously down the moonlit street. While they were talking the wind had risen and clouds were scudding overhead. The huge eucalyptus trees tossed and moaned in the breeze, sending strangely shaped shadows skittering across the road. At the far end of the crescent she could just make out Rob's tall, powerful figure, hunched over, hands in pockets, striding along at a furious pace. A sudden cold fear took hold of her. He had been awfully upset about the baby this afternoon, and then there was this row with Miranda. Surely he wasn't really so depressed that he would take her crazy suggestion seriously? Jo looked up the road again, and saw that the dark figure had vanished. She began to run.

'Rob!' she shouted. 'Rob, wait!'

It was ten minutes before she caught him up. By then her breath was coming in painful gasps and her legs felt like cotton wool. But as she came out on to the rugged hillside at the edge of the town she saw his tall, strong figure outlined unmistakably on the skyline above the dark, yawning chasm of the Super Pit. A shaft of pure terror went through her, and she launched herself across the final stretch of road like a wild creature.

'Don't do it, Rob!' she shrieked, flinging herself on him and grabbing the rough denim of his jacket. 'It's not worth it!'

'Jo, what are you talking about?' demanded Rob in a voice of pure bewilderment.

Tugging furiously at his clothes, she tried to haul him away from the edge.

'Miranda didn't mean it, Rob!' she babbled. 'I know she didn't. And you'll feel differently about the baby in the morning. Oh, please, Rob, come away. . .'

She paused, suddenly aware of the fact that she was clinging to his taut, muscular body, and he wasn't pushing her away. He wasn't trying to make a final, wild lunge for the edge, and he wasn't struggling to escape. In fact, a faint, disbelieving smile seemed to be spreading across his moonlit features.

'Jo,' he said in a voice that was deep and vibrant with amusement. 'You don't seriously believe that I came up here tonight so I could jump off the edge, do you?'

Jo's hold on his jacket slackened.

'You mean you weren't thinking about. . .?'

She waved one hand at the two-hundred-foot drop below them, and stopped uncertainly. Rob stared at her in disbelief.

'No,' he said at last. 'I was actually thinking about how much I'd like to wring Miranda's neck, but never mind about that now. Did you really come up here to save me?'

Jo took a long, shuddering gulp of air, and nodded.

'Yes,' she admitted bluntly.

Rob threw back his head and roared with laughter. A vigorous, cheerful sound that was overwhelmingly reassuring. And also intensely embarrassing.

'It's not funny!' protested Jo indignantly, her shoulders still heaving as she fought for breath. 'I went the wrong way, and ran into a cul de sac. I must have covered a mile and a half to get here, and I skinned my knuckles on a fence at the last corner. And all you can do is stand there and laugh!'

'Oh, Jo,' said Rob tenderly. 'You're one of a kind, you really are!'

Still fighting back his laughter, he took her hand and led her away from the brink of the Super Pit. Then he lifted up her fingers and peered at the injured knuckles in the moonlight.

'Well, that doesn't look too serious,' he pronounced teasingly. 'Shall I kiss it better for you?'

Jo's eyes flashed angrily and her chin jutted out. Although she didn't realise it she made a magificent picture against the harsh backdrop of the ruined landscape with the moonlight turning her hair to molten silver. Suddenly Rob caught his breath, and his fingers tightened on her arms.

'Yes, I think I will,' he murmured huskily.

His voice was no longer amused, but filled instead with a vibrant passion that sent a quiver of longing through Jo's entire body. Then he dragged her hard up against him and kissed her, so that the quiver became a raging torrent of desire. His hands were warm and hard and merciless, raking her long curls away from her face and turning her mouth imperiously up to his. But his kisses were sheer ecstasy. Long and deep and unbearably exciting, while the powerful thrust of his body against hers, the sheer, urgent male strength of his warmth against her, was irresistible. Jo took a swift, shuddering breath, and kissed him back. Hard. She heard his faint groan of disbelief and delight, then his hands moved down over her body, pressing and squeezing and moulding her against him, until they were so closely locked together that she could feel the frantic thud of his heartbeat through her thin shirt. Fire seemed to leap through her veins at his touch, and she felt dizzy and exhilarated as his mouth plundered hers.

But of course it had to end. While she was still yielding

Take 4 Medical Romances

Mills & Boon Medical Romances capture all the excitement and emotion of a busy medical world... A world, however, where love and romance are never far away.

We will send you 4 MEDICAL ROMANCES absolutely FREE plus a cuddly teddy bear and a mystery gift, as your introduction to this superb series.

At the same time we'll reserve a subscription for you to our Reader Service.

Every month you could receive the 4 latest Medical Romances delivered direct to your door postage and packing FREE, plus a free Newsletter filled with competitions, author news and much more.

And remember there's no obligation, you may cancel or suspend your subscription at any time. So you've nothing to lose and a world of romance to gain!

FREE

Your Free Gifts!

Return this card, and we'll send you a lovely little soft brown bear together with a mystery gift... So don't delay!

Reader Service
FREEPOST
P.O. Box 236
Croydon
CR9 9EL

SEND NO MONEY NOW

FREE BOOKS COUPON

YES Please send me 4 FREE Medical Romances, together with my teddy bear and mystery gift. Please also reserve a special Reader Service subscription for me. If I decide to subscribe, I will receive 4 brand new books for just £5.80 each month, postage and packing free. If, however, I decide not to subscribe, I shall write to you within 10 days. The free books and gifts will be mine to keep in anycase. I understand that I am under no obligation - I may cancel or suspend my subscription at any time simply by writing to you. I am over 18 years of age.

EXTRA BONUS

We all love mysteries ...so as well as your FREE books and teddy bear, here's an intriguing gift especially for you... No clues - so send off today!

9A1D

Mrs/Miss/Ms _____

Address _____

_____

_____

Postcode _____ Signature _____

Offer expires 31st December 1991. The right is reserved to refuse an application and change the terms of this offer. Readers overseas and in Eire please send for details. Southern Africa write to Independent Book Services, Postbag X3010, Randburg 2125. You may be mailed with offers from other reputable companies as a result of this ☐

blissfully to his caresses he suddenly gave a ragged gasp and thrust her purposefully away. His breath was coming fast and shallow as if he were the one who had been running. He uttered a soft groan, and then clutched her arms again.

'I won't say I'm sorry,' he said urgently. 'Because I'm not. But if I don't stop now I won't be able to. Will you come for a walk with me, and give us both a chance to cool down?'

Jo nodded breathlessly, and a tiny shiver, whether of cold or reaction, ran through her body.

'Here, take my jacket,' Rob ordered roughly, whipping it off and flinging it round her shoulders. 'You'll freeze if you're not careful.'

Jo became aware of the tiny stinging particles of dirt that were blowing off the tailings dump at the edge of the pit and striking her bare arms. She clutched the jacket instinctively around her and inhaled deeply, conscious of the aroma of Rob's French cologne mingled with the faint, wild tang of his own warm body.

'What about you?' she murmured.

His perfect white teeth gleamed in the moonlight.

'I'll survive,' he replied. 'I'm tough.'

They walked for five minutes along the perimeter of the Super Pit without speaking. But at last Jo broke the silence.

'Well, if you weren't going to jump over the edge, what did you come up here for?' she demanded.

Rob gave a wry chuckle, and came to a halt.

'Good question,' he said. 'And I don't really know how to answer it. I left Tom's place because I was coming close to exploding and I didn't want to have a full-scale argument with Miranda in public. As for why I came up here, that's a bit more complicated. I've been making pilgrimages up this hillside since I was a boy.'

'It does have a very nice view of the town. . .' said Jo

uncertainly, looking down at the light strung out below them like decorations on a Christmas tree.

'Oh, yes,' agreed Rob heavily. 'But that's not the view I come for. It's this one over here.'

He took her by the shoulders and swung her round to face the moonlit ridge outside the town. Against the bright, white radiance of the sky, the headframe above the mine shaft stood out like some monstrous, giant Meccano set.

'But. . .that's just the entrane to the mine shaft,' remarked Jo in bewilderment.

'Yes, I know,' admitted Rob soberly. 'But it's also a kind of memorial to me. You see, my parents are down there somewhere buried under all those tons of rock. They never did find the bodies.'

He spoke without self-pity, but Jo caught the aching undertone in his voice.

'Oh, Rob,' she said, hugging him spontaneously. 'I'm so sorry.'

For an instant he held her pressed against him, his cheek resting on the top of her head. Then his lips touched her hair.

'Well, I shouldn't be making a fuss about it,' he murmured. 'It was all so long ago.'

Jo glanced up and saw the faraway look in his eyes and the deep, unresolved pain that still lingered in his face. Sensing his need to talk, she prompted him gently.

'How did it happen?'

Rob sighed.

'We. . .were only up here on a visit,' he began slowly. 'You see, Tom was about fifteen years older than my father and, although they both grew up in Kalgoorlie, Dad won a scholarship to the medical school in Perth. He became a doctor, met my mother, and settled there. But in the meantime Tom had made his big find on the goldfields. A few years after the first nugget was discovered he sank a second shaft. That's the one you can see across there. We were invited for the opening, and on the day before it my parents went down for a preview of one of the new tunnels with the mine foreman. There was a big rock fall. . .and that was that.'

Jo's face twisted in sympathy.

'How did you ever bear it?' she asked.

Rob shrugged.

'Well, I was only five years old at the time,' he said. 'And I don't suppose I fully grasped what had happened. But there's no doubt that it left its mark. In a strange way I felt as if everything I loved was wiped out, and all I got in return was this useless stream of gold that kept coming out of the shaft. I've hated Rainbow End and the mine ever since.'

'Hated it?' echoed Jo. 'That's a very strong word to use.'

'Strong, but true,' countered Rob frankly. 'Oh, don't get me wrong. I think the people here are the salt of the earth. Generous, down to earth, hardworking, full of humour. But if I could walk out of the place tomorrow and never come back I'd be delighted.'

He spoke with such vehemence that Jo stared at him in astonishment.

'Then why don't you?' she demanded.

It was Rob's turn to look astonished.

'How the hell can I?' he retorted fiercely. 'It would break Tom's heart. I'm enough of a disappointment to him as it is. I know he always wanted me to become a mining executive instead of a doctor, but at least as a GP here I can keep an eye on him and show an interest in the mine, however much I dislike it.'

'I think that's utterly ridiculous!' exclaimed Jo bluntly.

Rob looked annoyed. 'You seem to forget that he's a very sick, old man,' he pointed out. 'It would be heartless just to abandon him. He needs looking after.'

'Sick! Old!' said Jo contemptuously. 'Have you got any other threadbare excuses for not having the courage to live your own life?'

'Now, just a minute——' began Rob warningly.

'And as for heartless,' cut in Jo, 'I think it's much more heartless to make that poor old man live with the guilt of worrying about whether he's ruining your life. He probably already feels responsible for your parents' death, and that's quite enough guilt for one person to carry around. So why don't you just go ahead and do what you really want to do?'

Rob paused with his mouth open.

'Anyway, what do you want to do?' finished Jo curiously.

'Be an obstetrician in Perth,' replied Rob without hesitation.

Jo grinned. 'Well, do it, then,' she urged.

'It's not that simple——' began Rob, but Jo interrupted him again.

'Isn't it?' she challenged.

He stroked his chin thoughtfully, and a slow smile spread over his face.

'You know, you're really something, Jo,' he said wonderingly. 'It's a damned good thing you didn't go into mining administration. You would have steam-rollered everything in your path!'

'But why don't you think about getting an obstetrics post in Perth, if that's what you really want?' persisted Jo. 'Tom is a really nice old man, and I'm sure he'd wish you well.'

Rob smiled non-committally.

'Well, maybe I will,' he conceded. 'But look, Jo. We've spent all this time talking about me and what I want, but how about you? I really know nothing about you. What do *you* want out of life?'

Jo shrugged and smiled.

'Nothing very complicated,' she said. 'A job that I like. Friends.'

'A husband? Children?' quizzed Rob.

'Oh, yes,' said Jo softly. 'One of these days, if I'm lucky.'

She turned away her face, conscious even in the moonlight of the slow flush that was spreading over her cheeks. It was madness, that thought she had had in the shower today about marrying Rob. Why in a million years would he ever want to marry a girl like her? And, as if to confirm her realisation, he said something that made her flinch.

'I asked Miranda to marry me last year,' he remarked.

Jo was startled by the sudden flare of antagonism that surged through her. I hate that woman, she thought savagely. But somehow she fought down her turmoil.

'Did you?' she replied neutrally. 'What did she say?'

'Well, she didn't exactly turn me down flat,' continued Rob. 'But she said she couldn't see much point in it since she didn't want children and she needed to be free to move around for the sake of her career. Although she did hint that she might change her mind eventually.'

'So where does that leave you?' asked Jo.

Rob gave a harsh laugh. 'I wish to God I knew,' he answered. 'I know what I want. Marriage, a home, children, a wife who's with me, not permanently in orbit round the planet chasing contracts and mergers. But I suppose I'll just have to hope that she changes her mind one of these days.'

Jo felt a dull ache settle in the region of her heart.

'Yes, I suppose so,' she said in a subdued voice. 'As long as you're sure that Miranda is the woman you really want.'

'Oh, there's no question about that,' insisted Rob passionately. 'I think I fell in love with her from the first moment I saw her.'

'Oh,' said Jo. 'How wonderful.'

'Yes, it was,' agreed Rob. 'Look, I suppose we should be getting back now. Tom's guests will probably have left by now, and I don't like to leave him alone for too long. But thanks for listening, Jo. I've never really been able to discuss these things with anybody else before.'

'You're welcome,' replied Jo listlessly.

It was after eight-thirty when they arrived home. The housekeeper had tidied up after the party and gone home, leaving Tom sitting contentedly on a sun-lounger next to the pool with a drink at his elbow. As Rob and Jo came in through the gate, he raised his glass and saluted them.

'Here's mud in your eye!' he said challengingly.

Jo smiled.

'I hope you haven't had any alcohol,' she chided.

'Just the one,' replied Tom with a knowing wink. 'You couldn't find me a bag of potato crips to go with it, could you, me darlin'?'

'Just this once!' replied Jo in martyred tones, going into the kitchen.

She reappeared a moment later with a large pink and black plastic bag, which made Rob frown disapprovingly.

'Potato crisps are loaded with cholesterol,' he pointed out.

'Not these,' said Jo, waving the bag. 'I bought the cholesterol-free type just for Tom.'

'Good on yer, love!' cried Tom. 'If I was thirty years younger, I'd ask yer to marry me!'

'If you were thirty years younger, I'd say yes!' retorted Jo, handing him the crisps with a smile.

Rob's entire body seemed to stiffen, and his blue eyes glittered angrily.

'Don't you think the car and the trip to Hawaii were enough?' he demanded.

Tom paused with his hands on the corner of the packet.

'What car? What trip?' he said slowly. 'Have you bin out in the sun too long today, Bob?'

Rob cast a startled look from Tom to Jo, who had suddenly become very engrossed in examining the foliage on a crimson bougainvillaea on the pergola. An unwelcome suspicion began to form in his brain.

'You mean. . .?' he muttered.

Tom's shrewd old eyes tracked from one to the other. Then he gave a sudden hoot of laughter.

'She's bin windin' you up, mate!' he said. 'And you fell for it, hook, line and sinker!'

CHAPTER FIVE

'RIGHT,' said Rob in a hard voice. 'You've had it, sweetheart!'

'W-what are you going to do?' quavered Jo nervously.

'Something I should have done two weeks ago,' he retorted grimly.

He advanced on her relentlessly, his blue eyes alight with laughter. She saw his swift glance towards the swimming pool and, with a despairing giggle, ducked behind Tom's sun-lounger.

'Oh, no!' she wailed. 'No, Rob! No, no, please, please, please! Ow, you beast!'

For, as she darted out from the other side of the sun-lounger, Rob leapt to block her way. His arms came round her, and she felt the muscles tighten like steel cables as he swept her off the ground. His breath fanned her cheek, and she could feel the thudding of his heart as he strode across the patio with her writhing body firmly pinioned against him.

'Put me down!' she shrieked, flailing at his chest with her fists.

'Oh, I will!' he promised silkily, holding her poised above the blue waters of the pool.

'No, not like that! Oh, you wretch, Rob! I'll get you for this! H-e-l-p!'

She hit the water with a resounding smack, and went under in a cascade of bubbles. Fortunately Jo was an excellent swimmer, and pure devilment suggested a fitting revenge. With a graceful twist she duckdived to the bottom of the pool and lay there holding her breath. A moment later there was another resounding splash as a second body hit the water. Then frantic hands caught in her clothes and dragged her to the surface. Treading water, she took a swift gulp of air and burst out laughing.

'Tricked you!' she cried triumphantly.

'You little demon!' exclaimed Rob, gazing at her with relief. 'That was a totally irresponsible thing to do! I thought I'd drowned you.'

Jo flung back her wet hair, and swallowed a grin. Paddling into shallower water, she stood up.

'Well, you *could* have drowned me!' she retorted pertly.

'Not you!' said Rob. 'I know you swim like a fish. I've seen you every morning.'

'Well, if we're talking about being totally irresponsible,' insisted Jo primly, 'throwing me into the pool was a pretty irresponsible thing to do, wasn't it?'

'I know!' groaned Rob. 'It's just that a kind of insanity seems to come over me when I'm with you. You're not really hurt, are you?'

He swam after her, and rose to his feet so that he could gaze anxiously into her face. Jo relented and shook her head. Her laughter rang out across the water.

'I'm fine,' she assured him. 'I only did it to make you get wet too.'

His answering laugh was deep and throaty, amazingly contagious. And his white teeth glistened against the full, sensual curve of his mouth before he suddenly bent his head and kissed her.

'You little minx,' he breathed.

Tiny ripples of excitement seemed to be lapping all through Jo's body. For an instant she stood motionless, intensely conscious of the touch of Rob's powerful thighs against hers, of the silky caress of the water flowing between her legs, of the sudden blaze of desire in his face. She looked down at her own body and saw that her T-shirt was clinging to her, revealing the hard, aroused points of her nipples. Blushing, she slid down below the water-line, and tried to hide her confusion.

'I think we'd better call a halt to this,' said Rob in an odd voice.

Heaving himself out of the pool, he crouched on the edge and held out one lean brown hand to Jo.

'Come on!' he ordered.

His arm was amazingly powerful, hauling her out of the water as effortlessly as if she were a child. In a moment she found herself sitting on the tiled edge, still holding his hand, and oblivious of the cool night breeze which was blowing a scattering of eucalyptus leaves across the patio. Oblivious of everything but the dark-haired man who crouched beside her.

'Enjoy your dip, did you?' said a familiar voice.

Jo started. She had forgotten all about Tom.

'Yes, thank you,' she replied with a grin that crinkled her freckled nose and made her tawny eyes dance laughingly. 'But I hope I didn't frighten you too, Tom.'

'No, no, love. I knew you was only doin' it for a bit of devilment, and I got a good laugh out of it. Better than a flamin' circus livin' with you two, and that's a fact! Still, I'm gettin' tired now, so I'll say goodnight, if you'll excuse me.'

'Yes, of course,' agreed Jo remorsefully. 'I'll come in and see that you're settled as soon as I'm dry.'

Left alone with Rob, Jo found herself feeling unaccountably shy, particularly since Rob was staring at her with his arms folded and an intent, thoughtful expression on his face.

'What is it?' she asked hesitantly.

'Nothing,' he said abruptly. 'I was just thinking that I like you better every minute that I spend with you. Goodnight, Jo.'

When Jo came into the kitchen the following morning she found Tom sitting alone at a table covered with a blue checked cloth. He had a newspaper propped against the cornflakes packet, and his lips were moving soundlessly as he scanned the financial pages.

'Good morning, Tom,' said Jo brightly, sitting

opposite him and unfolding her checked napkin. 'Did you sleep well?'

'Hmm? Eh? Oh, no, not real good. I was thinkin' too much. But never mind about that. Listen to this. This bloke Harrison reckons the chart of gold prices is beginnin' to look bullish. Yer see on the graph here? Gold in Australian dollars has been on a risin' trend, bouncin' off line B since 1982, then it goes into this here sideways pattern from 1982 to 1986, breaks upwards, forms a double-headed top through to 1988 and collapses back to line A. But it looks like she's risin' again. What do you reckon?'

'Oh,' said Jo blankly. 'I don't really know.'

Tom gave a sudden guffaw, and tossed the newspaper down on the table.

'You don't understand a word of that, do you, love?' he demanded. 'Never mind. Let's talk about somethin' you do understand. By all accounts you've been takin' the mickey out of Bob somethin' terrible. Now why would a nice girl like you do a thing like that?'

Tom looked at her severely over the tops of his bifocals. His blue eyes were no less shrewd for being old, and Jo found herself flushing under their piercing scrutiny. What if Rob came in and overheard this? She darted an anguished glance at the kitchen door.

'You don't need to worry about him,' said Tom crisply. 'He's already gorn off on his hospital rounds. There's only you and me here, and I'm just a nosy old man. But I would like an honest answer. Why did you tell him all that guff about a car and a trip to Hawaii?'

Jo looked nervously at Tom, but there was no sign of censure in the old man's face. Only a steady, patient curiosity. Her wild-rose colour slowly faded.

'I lost my temper,' she admitted. 'When I first met Rob he seemed convinced that I'd only helped you the day of your heart attack because you were wealthy. And then you offered me the job nursing you, and he thought I only wanted it because I was a gold-digger. He told

me so to my face. I was so furious I decided to play
along with him and really annoy him. So I told him the
most dreadful pack of lies about all the goodies you were
giving me. I'm sorry, Tom! I didn't mean to upset you
like this!'

The old man had hidden his face in his hands and his
shoulders were shaking. Jo jumped up in alarm and ran
to him, but as he raised his head she saw that tears of
laughter were streaming down his cheeks.

'By gum, you're a corker, young Jo!' he chuckled.
'That'll teach Bob to jump to conclusions! He's always
been a damned fool about the money from the mine.
Doesn't want it himself, but thinks everybody else is
after it!'

Jo smiled hesitantly. 'Th-then you're not angry?' she
faltered.

'Angry? No, not a bit of it,' denied Tom. 'Now you sit
down and have your breakfast, love.'

Jo went over to the gleaming marble counter-top, and
popped some bread in the toaster. Then she poured
herself a glass of orange juice. Before long she was sitting
opposite Tom again, thoughtfully spreading marmalade
on the hot, fragrant toast.

'I really am sorry,' she said again.

The old man gazed at her steadily. Then a slow smile
spread over his weather-beaten face, making him look
astonishingly like Rob.

'There's no need,' he assured her. 'I'm just glad it's
all sorted out, and I hope you and Bob can be friends
now.'

'I hope so, too,' agreed Jo.

'You know, Bob's a good bloke, none better, but he
takes life far too serious,' went on Tom. 'It'll do him
good to have a live wire like you around the place. A lot
more good than that flamin' Miranda does with all her
fancy airs and graces.'

Jo was startled by the intensity in his tone.

'Don't you like Miranda?' she asked curiously.

Tom heaved a deep sigh.

'She's a real smart lawyer,' he conceded. 'I wouldn't have hired her in the first place if she hadn't uv been, but she's the kind that's a damned sight too smart. She never sees nothin' but how we can cut costs and raise profits. I don't reckon she cares about the miners the way me and Bob do. Still, I suppose it won't do no harm if he's just havin' a bit of a fling with her. But, by cripes, I hope he won't marry the girl!'

Jo swallowed hard, feeling as if the toast had just turned to cardboard in her throat.

'Do you think he will?' she asked miserably.

Tom stroked his stubbly chin thoughtfully.

'Hard to say,' he conceded. 'A man can do some damned stupid things when he's lonely. And Bob's had a pretty lonely life since his parents died. Me and Bet did our best, but we were too old to be much company for him, and of course he's never liked Rainbow End. He always blamed the mine for his parents' death, and he never wanted anything to do with it. I hoped he'd grow out of that, but he never did. All he ever wanted was a career in medicine, and I can't say I blame him. In fact I'm real proud of the way he got his degree and his obstetrics certificate and everything. But what beats me is why he came back here to Rainbow End. He was doin' real well in Perth, you know—had a job that he loved in one of them big hospitals—and then he went and chucked it all in about three years ago to come and work as a GP in a mining town. What worries me, love, is that I'm afraid he done it all for me. You see, it was a bad time for me back then. My wife Bet had just died, I'd had me first heart attack, and I had some other problems what I won't go into. Well, Bob's a loyal sort of bloke, and I reckon he took it into his head that I needed him up here. He won't admit to it, mind you, but I'm sure that's it, and it makes me feel pretty crook, I can tell you. I feel as if I'm ruinin' his life, and that's the last thing I want to do. I wish he'd just move back to Perth and be done with it, if that's what he wants.'

Jo gazed at him, astounded. 'Wouldn't you mind?' she asked.

Tom smiled. A slow, sweet smile with a touch of sadness.

'I'd miss him,' he admitted. 'But I won't last much longer, love, I know that. And the finest thing I could have before I go is to see Bob married with a family of his own and doin' the job that he loves. That ud be worth more than a hundred gold mines to me!'

Jo bit her lip. She was touched by Tom's obvious concern for his nephew, but she wasn't blind to the facts. If Rob married anybody there would be no prizes for guessing who the bride would be. Sooner or later Miranda Sinclair would tire of playing with him and reel him in. Impatiently Jo rose to her feet, scooped up her dishes, rinsed them and stacked them in the dishwasher. Then she reached for Tom's empty bowl and cup.

'Yes, well I suppose Rob will marry when he's ready,' she said jauntily. 'But in the meantime I think I'd better check your blood pressure, Tom. And after that I've got some accounts to do for the surgery.'

Tom meekly allowed himself to be led away to his spacious suite overlooking the garden, where Jo fitted a cuff around his arm and pumped up the mercury. To her disquiet there was a small but significant rise in his blood pressure. One hundred and eighty-five over one hundred and ten. Frowning, Jo entered the results on the chart which she kept pinned to the foot of his bed.

'Your blood pressure's up a bit today, Tom,' she told him. 'Nothing too drastic at the moment, but it would be wise to take it easy. You've got a meeting later on, haven't you?'

'Yep. Two o'clock,' agreed Tom. 'Some of the company lawyers and accountants are coming over to discuss the new superannuation scheme.'

'Well, have a rest first,' advised Jo. 'And I'll look in and check you again before they arrive.'

When Jo tapped on Tom's door at twelve-thirty she found him peacefully leafing through a copy of *The Australian Stock Exchange Journal*. Methodically she took his pulse, checked his blood pressure again, wrote up the results, and patted him reassuringly on the arm.

'That looks a bit better,' she said. 'Now, will you be all right if I pop down to the surgery with these accounts for Margaret? They've been flat out down there with this gastro outbreak, and I know she wants to send these off today.'

'I'll be right as rain,' Tom reassured her. 'Anyway, Mrs Binns will be here vacuuming and what-not. She can give you a buzz if we need you.'

When Jo entered the waiting-room ten minutes later she found herself surrounded by a cluster of pale-faced, crying children and anxious looking mothers. In the centre of the chaos a harassed-looking Margaret Buckland was mopping the floor with one hand while she held the telephone with the other.

'Oh, Penny, not you too?' she was saying. 'No, don't worry about us. We'll manage somehow. I'll just have to cancel tomorrow's session if you can't make it. Now remember, plenty of fluids and nothing to eat for twenty-four hours. Bye.'

She dropped the receiver, set down the mop and blew out a long sigh. Then she caught sight of Jo.

'Are those the accounts?' she asked. 'Oh, bless you, Jo! It's been utter pandemonium in here this morning. I think half the kids in the town are down with gastro, and our child health clinic nurse has just phoned to say she's got it too. She's had to leave a health session at the primary school and go home, poor thing!'

The phone shrilled again.

'Here, let me!' said Jo.

She took the mop and bucket from Margaret and finished cleaning the floor. Then she took the implements out to the laundry at the rear of the surgery and left them to soak in disinfectant. After washing her hands, she stepped out into the corridor and stood for a moment looking up towards the waiting-room. Every instinct she had as a nurse urged her to go back and volunteer to help. She was still standing there when the door of the consulting-room opposite her opened and a worried-looking woman carrying a toddler came out, followed by Rob.

'Goodbye, Mrs Mather,' he said. 'Now remember, you can call me any hour of the day or night if you're anxious about Paul. Don't be frightened of disturbing me. That's what I'm here for.'

Suddenly he caught sight of Jo, and his face lit up.

'Hello,' he said. 'What are you doing here?'

'I just brought some accounts in for Margaret,' explained Jo. 'But I can't help feeling I ought to stay and help. It looks as if you're snowed under here.'

'It has been pretty desperate,' admitted Rob with a wry grin. 'But I'll tell you what you could do if you want to help.'

'What's that?' asked Jo.

'Drop in at the hospital and see how Janet Crabtree is getting on. I wanted to go myself, but it doesn't look as if I'll be getting a lunch-hour at this rate.'

'Yes, of course!' agreed Jo swiftly. 'I wanted to see her, anyway.'

'Thanks,' said Rob fervently.

His hand rested on her shoulder. It wasn't much, but that ordinary contact sent a surge of emotion through Jo. She looked into his cornflower-blue eyes and his preoccupied face, and a sense of love, pure and simple, welled up inside her. I need you, Rob, she thought. It was all she could do to stop herself from saying it aloud.

'What is it?' he asked.

'Nothing,' she replied hastily.

'I'll see you tonight, then.'

It was just after lunchtime when Jo reached the

hospital. A nurse knocked on the door of a pleasantly furnished private ward painted in pastel shades of blue and lilac, and then showed her in. Janet was lying huddled on her side with her back to the door, and she made no movement as they came in.

'Mrs Crabtree?' said the nurse hesitantly. 'There's a visitor for you.'

For a moment Jo thought that Janet must be asleep, but as she came around the foot of the bed and saw her face she realised that the other woman was simply staring blankly at the wall. A plate of ham salad lay untouched on a tray on the bed-table. Silently Jo sat down in the visitor's chair and waited. The nurse flashed her a crooked smile, and slid quietly out the door. The silence seemed to lengthen out and fill the room until Jo was intensely conscious of the steady beating of her own heart and the muted whirr of the air-conditioning system. At last Janet withdrew her blank gaze from the wall and fixed it on Jo.

'If you tell me to cheer up and it's not really so bad I'll scream,' she said aggressively.

Jo looked down helplessly at the bunch of gold chrysanthemums she was clutching in her hands.

'I wasn't going to tell you that,' she said bluntly. 'I don't see how you can cheer up. If this had happened to me I'd be so angry and upset I just couldn't bear it.'

Janet closed her eyes for an instant.

'I am angry,' she said in a hard voice. 'And I can't bear it. And everybody keeps being so bloody cheerful about it, and saying there, there, you'll have another baby, but I don't want another baby. I want this one!'

Her eyes came open. No longer blank, but blazing with pain and anguish.

'Oh, God, Jo, it's so unfair!' she finished.

Jo dropped the chrysanthemums on the bedside locker, and took Janet's hand. Her own eyes filled with tears.

'I know,' she murmured huskily. 'I know. Oh, Janet, what on earth are you going through?'

'Do you know what's the worst thing?' asked Janet. A tear rolled down her cheek and dropped silently on to the pillow. She laughed shakily. 'It's the rabbits. I spent weeks stencilling a frieze of little green rabbits round the back bedroom for the new baby, and now there isn't going to be any baby. And I know I'll just crack up when I go home and have to look at those stupid. . .hateful. . .rabbits. Oh, Jo!'

Suddenly the tears which had been backing up for the last twenty-four hours were released in a violent storm of weeping. There was not much Jo could do. She held Janet's hand and listened and passed her tissues until at last Janet hauled herself up against her pillows, red-eyed and gasping. Her shuddering breaths slowly quietened, and she gave Jo a watery smile.

'I'm not much company today,' she said apologetically. 'But Bill and I are both grateful for what you and Rob did for us. You must come to dinner some time.'

'Thanks,' replied Jo sincerely. 'I'd like that.'

Then she drew the covers up over Janet and patted them into place.

'Why don't you have a rest now?' she suggested.

On the short walk home Jo was haunted by the memory of Janet's tear-stained face, but deep down she felt sure that the other girl would soon come to terms with her sorrow. Certainly Janet had suffered a painful loss, but she still had the most precious support that anybody could hope for. A loving husband who needed her and would see her through. Remembering the desperate anxiety in Bill Crabtree's face the previous day, Jo felt a sudden sharp pang of envy. Nobody cares about me like that, she thought. Then hot on the heels of that realisation came the poignant memory of Rob's kisses the previous evening. Kisses that were not merely throbbing with passion, but somehow searingly emotional as

well. For a few intoxicating minutes last night she had
felt as if she and Rob were united in an intense emotional
bond that could never be broken. Until Rob had ruined
everything by telling her about Miranda. Jo groaned
aloud. What a fool I am! she thought. If I had any sense
I'd leave right this minute and go back to Perth. But
poor old Tom would miss me, and somehow I can't bear
to let Rob go, even if we're never going to be anything
more than friends. Plucking a spray of peppercorns from
a trailing green tree, she crushed the berries absent-
mindedly between her fingers and inhaled their pungent,
spicy aroma. I'll stay another couple of weeks, she
decided. At least until Tom goes back to Perth for his
next cardiac examination.

When she reached the luxurious bungalow she found
everything very quiet. Peeping through Tom's open
bedroom door, she saw that he was sleeping peacefully,
so she tiptoed out again. In the kitchen a note on the
spotless table informed her that it was Mrs Binns's half-
day off and there was a casserole in the refrigerator for
dinner. Unable to think of anything else to do, Jo amused
herself by setting the dining-room table with the best
china and silverware, and arranging a crystal bowl of
flowers in the centre. Then she prowled around the
house looking for something useful to do. By the time
Tom awoke at five o'clock she had done a pile of
mending, sorted and labelled all the computer disks on
Rob's desk, and even tidied the huge cupboard which
occupied half of one wall in the study. This was quite a
feat, since it contained a horrifying jumble of patent
medicines, drug company catalogues, printer ribbons,
case notes scrawled on the back of old envelopes, and
articles about the Americas Cup Yacht Race. Jo felt a
glow of satisfaction as she closed the door on the
immaculate shelves and staggered away with a green
garbage bag full of rubbish. Even if Rob never appreci-
ated another thing she did, he would be grateful for this.

Jo made some tea, and she and Tom sat for an hour

or so drinking it and chatting about the old mining days
in Kalgoorlie and Tom's discovery of gold at Rainbow
End. By six-fifteen she was conscious of every car that
turned into the terrace, but there was still no sign of
Rob. Although the days were so hot, autumn nights in
the inland were remarkably chilly, and half an hour later
she gave up waiting for Rob, and lit the fire in the
sitting-room fireplace. Its orange flames crackled up
brightly, and Tom stretched his hands out gratefully to
the warmth.

'I reckon Bob's workin' late at the surgery,' he commented. 'Perhaps you better put the dinner in the oven
now, love. He don't like me to wait for him when he's
runnin' a bit late.'

Obediently Jo put the casserole in the oven, and soon
the rich aroma of stewed beef, mushrooms and jacket
potatoes filled the room. Tom suggested a drink to pass
the time, and Jo had just poured him an alcohol-free
beer and was tipping ice cubes into a glass for her own
gin and tonic when she heard the sound of a car in the
driveway. Hastily she filled another glass with ice, added
a generous measure of whisky and soda, and went into
the hall to greet Rob. He looked tired and dishevelled as
he flung open the front door, but a warm smile lit his
face as he saw Jo. Tossing his keys on to the hall table,
he set down a huge bunch of white roses beside them,
and loosened his tie.

'What a day!' he exclaimed. 'Do you think those roses
look all right?'

'They're gorgeous!' replied Jo, picking them up and
sniffing them ecstatically. 'Are they for Miranda?'

'No, they're for you,' replied Rob.

'For me?'

Jo was touched and startled. She ran a disbelieving
finger over one of the delicate white petals, and then
inhaled the strong, fruity fragrance of the flowers. A shy
smile flitted over her face, and her eyes were suddenly
as bright as stars.

'But why?' she demanded.

Rob smiled an engagingly mischievous and penitent smile.

'I thought I owed you an apology for my suspicions about your motives,' he admitted. 'So I decided to say it with flowers. Josephine Webster, I am very sorry for my dastardly behaviour, and I hope with all my heart that you'll forgive me.'

Jo grinned impishly. 'I'll think about it,' she retorted.

'Only think about it?' demanded Rob in an outraged voice. 'You'll do more than just think, my girl, or I'll know the reason why! And while we're on the subject of apologies, when are you going to apologise to me for all those appalling lies you told me?'

Jo cringed dramatically, and dropped to her knees.

'Oi be very sorry, sir!' she wailed. ''Tis me wicked lyin' tongue what does it, and oi don't know what come over me. Only say that you'll forgive me, and oi will be a better girl.'

Rob tangled his fingers in her long, tawny-brown curls and gazed laughingly down at her.

'I rather enjoy seeing you humble!' he said. 'It's a new experience. So what are you going to do to convince me of your true penitence, wicked girl?'

Jo scrambled to her feet, and darted into the kitchen.

'How about giving you a large whisky and soda?' she asked in her normal voice.

'Oh, Jo, you're a life-saver!' exclaimed Rob. 'I knew you had triple certificates in nursing, but I didn't realise one of them was for mind-reading.'

He took the glass and swallowed a large gulp of the drink.

'Bad day?' asked Jo.

'Atrocious,' he agreed. 'It's this wretched viral gastroenteritis. I had another dozen kids in the surgery with it today, and two of them were so bad I had to admit them to hospital. And the worst of it is that Penny Hughes, our child health sister, is down with the bug

too. That means that we'll have to cancel her clinic
tomorrow. I hate doing that at a time like this, because
a lot of the young mums in town just don't realise how
serious gastroenteritis can be for a baby. If the clinic is
open and they have a sick kid they'll often pop in to
Penny for advice, but they won't bother taking the child
to the doctor. It worries me a bit.'

'I could do her clinic tomorrow,' offered Jo. 'As long
as Tom doesn't mind being left.'

Rob's face brightened.

'Could you?' he said. 'I'd be grateful. Penny's funded
by the state health department, so I'd have to ring them
and clear it first, but I'm sure they'd only be too pleased
to have you.'

'Well, that's settled then,' agreed Jo calmly. 'How
were the rest of your patients today? Did you treat
anything other than gastroenteritis?'

Rob sighed.

'Nothing very dramatic,' he said. 'Mrs Clark came in
with another bad attack of sinusitis. Which reminds me,
I must just go into my study and check the specialist I
referred her to in Perth last time she had an attack.'

He moved purposefully towards the door of the study.

'I'll just go and put these flowers in some water,'
murmured Jo, heading for the kitchen.

A smug glow of anticipation coursed through her
veins. Well, even if Rob had had an awful day, he would
get a nice surprise when he saw his study looking so tidy
and efficient. Jo was just running water into a crystal
vase when there was a roar of outrage from the far end
of the hall.

'Just look what that woman has done!'

Jo rushed out of the kitchen, but had to flatten herself
against one wall as Rob went seething past like a lava-
flow in full spate. Nervously she followed him into the
sitting-room.

'Where is she?' he shouted.

'Who?' asked Tom placidly. 'Young Jo?'

'No, not Jo! That bloody cleaning woman. Mrs Binns! I've told her a thousand times not to touch that cupboard in my study, and what does she go and do? Turns the whole thing upside down so I can't find a damned thing in it! What's her telephone number? I'm going to ring her up and have a piece of her for this!'

Jo took a swift, deep breath, and stepped between Rob and the telephone.

'Just calm down, Rob!' she advised. 'It wasn't Mrs Binns who tidied up your cupboard. It was me.'

Rob treated her to a furious glare.

'You've got a nerve!' he exclaimed. 'I had a lot of important medical details in there, and now I can't find a thing!'

'I'm surprised you could find anything before, it was such a disgusting mess!' retorted Jo tartly. 'And there's no need for you to lose your temper! I've no intention of being spoken to like that, and, as for finding things, just follow me and I'll explain where everything is.'

'Well, the explanation had better be good,' grumbled Rob, following her along the hall and into the study. 'What about Mrs Clark's notes, for a start? I had them on the back of an airmail envelope in the tin of thumb-tacks on the top shelf.'

'No, you didn't,' contradicted Jo. 'They were in the bottom of that revolting box of dried-up cough syrups on the second top shelf underneath your soldering iron.'

'Did you find my soldering iron?' asked Rob with sudden interest. 'I've been looking for that for weeks.'

Mutely Jo reached into a box of mixed hardware in the cupboard and produced the soldering iron.

'Yes, well,' continued Rob hastily. 'That's very nice, but what about Mrs Clark's case notes?'

'I threw them out,' said Jo.

'You what?' roared Rob.

'Oh, for heaven's sake!' exclaimed Jo. 'I entered all the information on to the computer data base first, and I'm going to take it in to the surgery tomorrow and add it to the records there. But it just seemed absolutely ridiculous to me to keep all those scraps of paper lying around in such a jumble. I don't know how you could find anything.'

There was a long pause.

'Actually, I've been meaning to put all that stuff on computer myself,' admitted Rob. 'But I've never had the time to do it. Are you sure you can find the information again, though?'

Jo's only answer was to switch on the computer. There was a sudden ding, then she inserted a disk and clicked twice on the mouse. Bending over the computer, she typed in CLARK, MARY FRANCES, and pressed a key. Immediately an entry came up on the screen.

FILE NUMBER: 67392 CLARK, MARY FRANCES. D.O.B. 17 JANUARY, 1943. SINUSITIS. REF. DR P. BURGESS, SUITE 3, 115 CARLISLE STREET, PERTH, read Rob thoughtfully.

He stroked his chin.

'Hmm,' he growled. 'Perhaps I've been a bit hasty. You didn't throw out my Americas Cup clippings, though, did you?'

A slow smile spread over Jo's face.

'No, I didn't throw out your Americas Cup clippings,' she reassured him. 'They're in that blue folder on the bookcase.'

Rob caught the twinkle in her eye, and his fierce dark eyebrows slowly relaxed. A reluctant grin hovered at the corners of his mouth, and he shrugged despairingly.

'All right, I'm a bad-tempered bear,' he admitted. 'Shall I buy you another bunch of flowers to say that I'm sorry?'

Jo showed him the tip of her pink tongue. 'I think you'd better,' she teased.

He put his arm around her and gave her a sudden, unexpected squeeze.

'Thank you for tidying up my horrible belongings,' he said. 'I don't know what I'd do without you. Now shall we go back and join Tom?'

Tom grinned knowingly as Rob made a meek return to the sitting-room.

'All sorted out?' he asked with a hint of sarcasm.

'Yes, thank you, Tom,' agreed Rob sardonically. 'Jo has everything under control, as usual.'

Silently Jo handed him his whisky-glass again, and he took a grateful gulp.

'This is very nice,' he said with a sigh, indicating the blazing fire and the attractive table-setting in the dining area. 'And something smells great. What is it?'

'Beef bourguignon, courtesy of Mrs Binns,' replied Jo. 'But I've done some jacket potatoes with sour cream and chives and a side dish of broccoli and carrots. And I made some of that lemon mousse that you said you liked.'

'Oh, Jo, I'm sorry!' exclaimed Rob remorsefully. 'I forgot to tell you. I can't eat here tonight. I promised to take Miranda out to dinner.'

Jo was silent for a moment, swallowing down the lump in her throat.

'It doesn't matter,' she assured him carelessly.

'I really am sorry,' insisted Rob, observing the forced smile that hid her disappointment. 'I would have enjoyed it immensely.'

After Rob's departure Jo and Tom ate their meal in silence. Then, pleading a headache which was more than half-genuine, Jo escaped to the privacy of her bedroom. She had just flung herself down on the apricot satin quilt when the phone rang. Jo hesitated. It was almost certainly for Tom, but he was a bit deaf and slow on his feet. She had better answer it.

'Good evening. Challender residence,' she said. 'Josephine Webster speaking.'

'Jo! You do sound posh!'

'Mary Lou! How nice to hear from you. Where are you calling from?'

'Perth,' said Mary Lou. 'And I'll have to make this quick. I've got to be at work in fifteen minutes, and one of the kids has just thrown a tin of pineapple chunks all over the kitchen floor. Listen, are you still interested in a job at St Jude's?'

Jo's head whirled and then cleared. She had a vision of Rob gazing soulfully across a candlelit dinner-table at Miranda.

'I might be,' she said cautiously. 'Why?'

'Well, I've just heard that one of their old hands is leaving. They'll be advertising the position in this Saturday's *Weekend Australian* and they want to fill it about a month from now. So look out for the advert if you're interested.'

'Thanks,' said Jo. 'I will.'

'Look, I must dash,' apologised Mary Lou. 'Give me a ring next time you're in Perth, and we'll have lunch or something. Bye.'

'Bye,' replied Jo thoughtfully, replacing the receiver.

As she drank her coffee in the child health clinic late the following afternoon Jo brooded over Mary Lou's suggestion. Really, it would be the best thing for her to make a clean break. In spite of his annoyance on the night of the party Rob didn't really seem to find the company of the lovely Miranda too hard to take. Last night, for instance, he hadn't arrived home until after two a.m. Obviously the smartest thing Jo could do was to leave Rainbow End and simply forget him. But why did that prospect fill her with such a terrible sense of despair? Shaking her head, Jo rinsed out her mug, straightened her cap, and opened the door of the waiting-room with a bright smile.

'Next, please,' she said.

The woman who ambled awkwardly into the examination room was about six months pregnant with a pale, exhausted face and dark shadows under her eyes. She was holding a little girl of about two with one hand, and dragging a six-year-old boy by the back of his T-shirt with the other. The boy pointed a stick at Jo.

'Bang! You're dead!' he cried loudly. Then he darted

across the room, clutched at his chest and let out a loud groan. 'A-a-a-a-r-g-h! She got me, Sheriff!'

With a couple of dramatic, staggering turns he fell on to his knees and then pitched forward on his face.

'Geoffrey!' cried his mother sharply. 'Stop that at once! Get up! Do you hear me?'

There was no response. With a weary sigh the mother waddled across to the prostrate figure, dragged the child to his feet, and slapped him sharply on the rear. Then she took the wooden gun and threw it in Jo's waste-paper basket.

'I'm sorry, Nurse,' she said despairingly. 'He's just driving me insane.'

'Don't worry,' replied Jo sympathetically, waving at a chair. 'Why don't you sit down and tell me what the problem is, Mrs——?'

'Hunter. Beth Hunter.'

Jo rummaged swiftly in the filing cabinet behind her desk.

'Right,' she said. 'And this must be Geoffrey? And Sarah? Well, what's the trouble? Is it this awful gastric bug that's going around?'

'No,' replied Mrs Hunter with a crooked smile. 'We've been lucky with that so far. No, it's Geoffrey. I'm starting to wonder if he's got some kind of mental problem, his behaviour is so weird. He used to do really well at school, but now his teacher says he's completely disruptive and falling behind with his work. And at home he's just as bad. All he wants to do is turn the television up on top volume or torment Sarah. And he never listens to a word I say when I tell him to do something.'

She cast a bitter glance at her son, who was busy playing with a pile of musical instruments on a side table. Already he had built a high tower of shakers, cymbals, tambourines and sleigh bells. As they watched he started to balance a drum precariously on the top.

'Geoffrey, stop that!' cried his mother.

But the child blithely continued to build until suddenly the entire structure fell to the floor with a spectacular crash so that little Sarah jumped and screamed with fright. Geoffrey just smiled sweetly.

'You naughty boy!' shouted his mother. 'Come here at once! Do you hear me?'

Jo laid a restraining hand on the distraught mother's arm.

'I don't think he does, Mrs Hunter,' she said gently.

'What do you mean?' demanded Beth Hunter sharply. Then her look of blank bewilderment changed suddenly to horrified comprehension. 'You don't mean. . . Geoffrey's deaf?'

'Look, don't panic before you need to,' urged Jo reassuringly. 'It's not uncommon for children to have temporary hearing loss, especially following a bad cold or ear infection. Has Geoffrey had anything like that in the last few months?'

Mrs Hunter sat down.

'Yes, he has actually,' she said slowly. 'He had a really bad dose of the flu about six or seven months ago. Do you really think it could have affected his hearing?'

'Well, it's certainly a possibility,' admitted Jo. 'Poor school work, turning the television up loud, not taking any notice when you talk to him all sound like classic symptoms.'

'Oh, no!' exclaimed Mrs Hunter guiltily. 'And here I've been slapping him and shouting at him.'

'Well, if we can get things sorted out you'll all feel the benefit of it,' said Jo comfortingly. 'But the first thing I'd like to do is check Geoffrey with the audiometry kit. If that shows any hearing loss I think you should take him to your GP to have him checked. Which doctor do you see, by the way?'

'Dr Challender,' replied Mrs Hunter in a worried voice. 'Do you think he'll be able to help him, though?'

'Almost certainly,' said Jo. 'This sort of condition often cures itself and, even if it doesn't, it's usually just a matter of a simple operation to insert grommets to drain the ears.'

'An operation?'

'It only requires an overnight stay in hospital. He'd have to go to Perth for it, but the State Government would pay his fare. And it may not even come to that. Let's check him first, shall we?'

But when Jo took out the audiometry kit, put the headphones on Geoffrey's head and tested his hearing on the various sound frequencies, it soon became apparent that the boy had quite a severe hearing loss.

'Well?' asked Mrs Hunter anxiously.

'He does seem to have a bit of a problem,' admitted Jo cautiously. 'I think you should book him in to the doctor right away, and I'll make sure that Dr Challender sees these audiogram results as soon as possible.'

'Thank you, Nurse,' said Mrs Hunter bleakly.

'Cheer up,' urged Jo. 'I'm sure it's not as serious as you think.'

When Mrs Hunter had left the surgery Jo went out into the waiting-room and looked around. To her surprise there were no more children to be seen and only a couple of adult patients on the long leather benches against the walls.

'Is Rob busy, Marg?' she asked.

Marg looked up and smiled. 'No, it's really slackened off, thank goodness,' she said. 'He's free if you need him, Jo.'

Jo tapped on Rob's door.

'Come in,' growled a surly voice.

Curiously Jo opened the door and went in. Rob glanced up sharply, and she saw that his face wore a smouldering expression.

'How was the dinner last night?' asked Jo, tempting fate.

'Don't ask!' snapped Rob. 'What can I do for you?'

Jo hid a smile. Perhaps Miranda hadn't been so lovely after all.

'One of your patients with suspected glue ear,' she said. 'He's coming back tomorrow to see you, but I think you should take a look at this audiogram first.'

They bent over the graph together, and Jo was conscious of a tiny thrill as Rob's brown hand brushed against hers. But, as always in working hours, Rob was strictly professional as they discussed the case.

'Well, let me know how he gets on, won't you?' asked Jo, when the shrilling telephone finally put an end to their conversation.

'Yes, of course,' agreed Rob, reaching for the phone. 'And thanks. You did well to spot this.'

On Saturday morning Jo was lounging by the pool when Rob came back from his morning surgery.

'Well, you were right about the Hunter boy,' he said, tossing a bundle of newspapers on to the lounger beside her. 'It was definitely glue ear. I'm going to wait a few weeks to see if it clears up spontaneously, but I can't say I'm really hopeful. I think he'll have to go to Perth to see a specialist, and it's ten to one he'll need grommets in the ears. Now, do you want a newspaper?'

Jo snatched eagerly at *The Weekend Australian*, and flicked through to the Hospital and Medical Appointments Section.

'Good, it's here!' she cried in triumph.

'What is?' demanded Rob.

'A position in paediatric nursing at St Jude's. I'm thinking of applying for it.'

Rob stared at her in horror.

'Don't be ridiculous!' he said sharply. 'How do you think we'd ever cope without you?'

CHAPTER SIX

Jo WAS silent for a moment, torn between exasperation and amusement.

'But you didn't even want me here in the first place,' she pointed out.

'I know,' admitted Rob with a groan, running his fingers through his gleaming black hair. 'But that's all changed, now that I know what you're really like. For heaven's sake, Jo, I told you I was sorry about jumping to conclusions. I think you're a great person, I really do. You're terrific company, always lively and full of pep, and yet when it comes to an emergency you're totally professional and nothing fazes you. I don't know how on earth I'd get along without you now.'

'Thanks,' muttered Jo, ducking her head and staring fixedly at a trail of ants in the red earth beside the patio. 'But I still think I ought to go.'

'Look at me, damn you,' ordered Rob in an aggrieved voice, putting one hand under her chin and raising it. 'I think you're one of the finest women I ever met. So why the hell are you getting in a huff and talking about leaving?'

Jo blinked, unable to stand up to the scrutiny of those deep, blue eyes.

'It's nothing to do with getting in a huff,' she protested, turning her gaze deliberately away to a flock of sulphur-crested cockatoos that were frolicking raucously in a gum tree. 'Nothing whatever to do with it.'

'So what is it to do with?' demanded Rob relentlessly. 'Tom thinks the sun shines out of you. He's going to be devastated if you leave him.'

'I know,' whispered Jo.

'Then why?' growled Rob.

Jo let out an exasperated cry.

'For an intelligent man you are an incredible fool sometimes, Rob!' she retorted, tossing her head and staring him straight in the eye. 'I'll tell you why I want to leave! It's because of Miranda.'

'Miranda! What's she got to do with it?'

Jo ground her teeth.

'Nothing!' she said savagely. 'Except that you're planning to marry her, and she might not be exactly overjoyed to learn that you were kissing me a couple of nights ago. And with every appearance of enjoyment, I might add. Maybe that sort of stuff doesn't matter to people like you. I wouldn't know, I don't belong to the jet set. But back where I come from they have a name for that kind of behaviour. It's called disloyalty.'

Rob sank into a chair. 'Go on,' he said in a taut voice.

'That's it,' shrugged Jo. 'If you want to know the truth I'm pretty disgusted by myself. Well, sure, it was only kissing, wasn't it? But believe it or not, Rob, kisses actually mean something to me. And I don't think I have a right to be kissing somebody else's man. So I'd rather be right out of the picture.'

Rob was silent, gazing at her with an intent, brooding look that made her yearn to reach out and touch him. But she screwed her fists into tight balls and kept them on her lap.

'Well, aren't you going to tell me how out of date and unliberated I am?' she demanded sourly, as the silence lengthened.

'No,' said Rob with a sigh. 'Much as I hate to admit it, I respect what you're saying. But, Jo, if I promised never to lay a finger on you again, couldn't you stay? Couldn't we just be friends?'

His lean brown hand smoothed back the tangled curls from her face, and he gazed earnestly into her tawny eyes. Jo gave a small, choking laugh, and her hand closed over his and moved it firmly away.

'Never to lay a finger on me?' she challenged. 'Oh,

Rob! You must see that it wouldn't work. If we stay under the same roof sooner or later the inevitable is going to happen. So either I'll have to leave or you will.'

As she said that her gaze strayed down to the newspaper that lay forgotten on her lap. A large advertisement caught her eye.

'But Jo——' began Rob.

'Rob!' exclaimed Jo in a different voice. A voice full of sudden excitement and enthusiasm. 'Maybe that's it. Maybe you ought to leave. Listen to this:

"A vacancy exists for an obstetrician to join a private obstetrics practice based in the central business district of Perth. Applicants should be qualified obstetricians holding the certificate of the R.A.C.O.G. with at least one year's post qualification experience in obstetrics. . ."

'Doesn't that sound exactly like what you want?'

'You mean move to Perth and take a job in obstetrics?' said Rob slowly.

'Yes! It's just what you've been longing for, isn't it?'

'I suppose it is,' Rob conceded, and there was an undertone of fierce longing in his voice. 'But it's no good. I couldn't leave Tom.'

'Of course you could!' insisted Jo. 'He thinks you should move to Perth. He told me so.'

'You mean you've been discussing me with Tom behind my back?' demanded Rob in outraged tones.

Jo flushed guiltily, and then rallied.

'Well, of course I have!' she retorted spiritedly. 'Discussing everybody else's business is the favourite occupation in Rainbow End—even bigger than gambling at Two-Up. Oh, don't be such a Puritan, Rob! Just read the advertisement and see what you think.'

She passed him the folded newspaper, and watched eagerly as he scanned it. There was no mistaking the growing excitement in his face.

'Did Tom really say I should move to Perth?' he asked.

'Yes,' insisted Jo. 'So what are you going to do?'

'For two pins I'd have a crack at this!' replied Rob. 'But I hate to just abandon the poor old bloke.'

'You wouldn't be abandoning him,' Jo insisted.

Rob sat back in his chair and heaved an impatient sigh.

'It's useless,' he said. 'Tom and I have always been really close. Well, not close in the sense of talking to each other much, I suppose, but I've always felt that when the chips were down I could rely on him through and through. And I'd like to think that he feels the same way about me. He's old and sick, and I don't feel that I can leave him. It would be a different matter if he had somebody else to rely on, somebody who was really fond of him.'

'I'm fond of him,' said Jo slowly.

Rob's startled blue eyes met hers, and an incredulous hope lit up his face for a moment. Then he flung the newspaper savagely on the ground.

'No, Jo!' he exclaimed. 'You're amazingly generous even to think of it, but I'd have no right to ask you to do it. I know perfectly well you want to go back to Perth and nurse children, not sit by Tom's bedside until the bitter end. It's not as though it's going to be easy, either. Even though Tom's hypertension is responding to treatment, I'm worried about all this coughing and breathlessness he's been suffering from. Whoever has to look after him from here on will be tackling a pretty hard job. And I'll be only too happy to stay with the old bloke. Honestly.'

Jo could not help admiring the way he hid his disappointment, but she saw his gaze stray almost unconsciously to the newspaper. Rising to her feet, she picked it up and held it out to him.

'It won't be any hardship to me,' she said steadily. 'I'm genuinely fond of Tom, you know that. And, to tell

you the truth, I was starting to feel quite badly about
the thought of leaving him. Why don't you phone them
about the position, Rob? You could probably go for an
interview while Tom's in Perth having his cardiac
examination. Then, if you get the job, you can stay on
in Perth and I'll come back to Rainbow End with Tom.
And if you don't it will be time enough then for me to
think about leaving him.'

Rob rose to his feet and took the newspaper from her
outstretched hand, but he didn't really look at it. Instead
he threw it on the chair, took her by the shoulders, and
looked down into her candid, golden eyes. His fingers
played with her tawny-brown curls, and his gaze lingered warmly on her features.

'All right, I will,' he agreed softly. 'But I want you to
know that you're the nicest woman I've ever met. Bless
you, Jo.'

'Nurse Webster?'

'Yes?'

Jo rose to her feet with a pleasant smile.

'Dr Lyall would like to see you about the results of Mr
Challender's cardiac examination, if you could just step
this way, please.'

Jo followed the receptionist down a pleasant, cream-
painted corridor fringed with lush green potted palms to
Dr Simpson's luxurious office. The cardiologist was
sitting at his huge mahogany desk with a large X-ray on
a screen behind his head.

'Ah, come in, Nurse Webster,' he greeted her amiably.
'Pleasant flight down from Rainbow End, I hope? Well,
I've just finished a very thorough battery of tests on
Tom Challender, and I'd like to discuss the results with
you, if I may.'

Something in the specialist's hearty tone made Jo's
spirits sink. She sat down in a chair and fixed her gaze
on him frankly.

'Is it bad news?' she asked in a composed tone, with only the faintest tremor to betray her concern.

'Not as good as we might have hoped,' admitted Dr Lyall with a sigh. 'I'm sure you're well aware of his symptons. Breathlessness, especially at night-time, swelling of the ankles, coughing up a lot of pink, frothy phlegm. Well, he's had a chest X-ray and an echo cardiogram, and I'm afraid there's no doubt about the results. Tom is suffering from an aneurysm of the heart.'

Jo gave him a horrified look. She knew perfectly well that a heart attack of the kind Tom had suffered frequently caused part of the heart muscle to die, so that the injured area then ballooned out to form an aneurysm. It was a serious condition, but in most cases surgery could be performed to repair the damage.

'Can't you operate?' she asked in dismay.

Dr Lyall shook his head regretfully.

'I'm afraid the aneurysm is inoperable,' he said, pointing to the X-ray on the wall behind him. 'You can see for yourself how large the shadowed area is, and Tom simply isn't a suitable candidate for surgery. The rest of his heart is so dicey he'd be very unlikely to survive an operation.'

'So, in other words, you think the end is very near for him?' Jo pressed.

'Well, as to that, I don't have a crystal ball,' replied Dr Lyall. 'But I'd have to say that I think we're looking at a life expectancy of months rather than years. Tom has asked me to explain all this to you and see what your response is to the idea of staying on as his private nurse. He's very keen to have you, but he doesn't want to burden you with the task of nursing a dying man if you're in any way unwilling. It can be a very depressing and exhausting job.'

Jo was silent, feeling a lump rising in her throat. She knew only too well how depressing and exhausting it could be. Hadn't she interrupted her training at the age of nineteen to nurse her mother to the bitter end of terminal cancer? But there was no question that mercy would always come first for Jo. She cleared her throat.

'I'll be glad to do it,' she said firmly.

Dr Lyall looked at her approvingly over the top of his glasses.

'I'm relieved to hear it,' he replied. 'Well, then, I'd suggest you take a well-earned break over the next few days. Even though I can't take the risk of operating, I may be able to relieve some of the symptoms with drug therapy. But I'll have to keep Tom in the clinic here for several days, so you might as well enjoy yourself until he's able to come home. I propose to put him on Captopril with a dosage of fifty milligrams three times a day, and two or three Frusemide tablets each morning. Of course, I must strees that the medication is only a palliative treatment, but it should have some effect on his symptoms.'

'Do you think he'll be fit enough to go back to Rainbow End, then?' asked Jo.

Dr Lyall shook his head.

'I'm afraid there can be no question of going back to Rainbow End,' he said firmly. 'Tom has completed all his business transactions now, and his most sensible course is to stay here in Perth, where he's close to good hospital facilities. He has some notion of giving a big party for his seventieth birthday next month, so that will give him something to look forward to. And I'm sure you'll be very comfortable at the house in Dalkeith.'

Jo was shown out with her thoughts in a turmoil. Very comfortable. Of course she would. Who wouldn't be comfortable in a thirty-room mansion with a river frontage in Millionaires' Row? She would be splendidly comfortable, if only it weren't for one thing. The fact that she would now be staying there alone with Rob Challender. Squaring her chin, she strode briskly in the direction of Dalkeith. Don't be ridiculous, Josephine Webster, she told herself sternly. This is not 1850, it is the late twentieth century, and there is no need to swoon

just because you're about to be Alone With A Man.
Anyway, you and Rob are just friends, remember?

When she reached Tom's house half an hour later she
strolled thoughtfully down through the garden, enjoying
the display of magnificent silver birches and Japanese
maples in their autumn colours, and humming softly to
herself. It was only one o'clock, far too early for Rob to
be home, and the prospect of a quiet afternoon lazing by
the river was tempting. She inserted her key in the door,
and then gave a muffled shriek as the door was suddenly
flung open and she found herself dragged inside and
swept into a passionate embrace. Urgent hands teased
out her neat chignon and sent her glorious curls tum-
bling riotously over her shoulders, then kisses rained
joyously on her eyes and cheeks and mouth. She caught
her breath, and then kissed wildly back.

'Rob!' she gasped at last. 'You beast! I thought you
were a cat burglar!'

His laugh was rich and velvety and resonant.

'Is that how you'd treat a burglar?' he demanded.
'Then I think I'll change my occupation! No, I won't! I
think I'm going to enjoy obstetrics too much.'

'Rob!' she shrieked. 'You mean, you got the job?'

'Yes!' he exclaimed exultantly. 'I got the job! Now get
changed right this minute, because I'm taking you out
for the best lunch you ever had in your life!'

Two hours later Jo sat gazing idly out at the surging
blue magnificence of the Indian Ocean at Fremantle. A
huge red, white and blue Cinzano umbrella protected
them from the fiercest rays of the sun, and red geraniums
split in a cascade down the yellow ochre wall of the
restaurant's balcony. In the background she could hear
the passionate outpouring of an Italian tenor singing
plaintive love songs, and on the table in front of her was
the debris of a superb meal. Crusty bread, black olives,
veal scaloppine, green salad, and the dregs of a bottle of
Houghton's White Burgundy. It was hard to remember
that she and Rob were only friends, especially when he

picked up her hand and smiled at her so intently.
Sighing, she withdrew her hand.

'Have you told Miranda about the job?' she asked
bluntly.

A shadow passed over his face.

'Yes,' he revealed. 'She didn't seem exactly overjoyed
about it. Although she did say that being in Perth would
give me a good chance to learn how the board of
Challender's operates.'

Jo struggled to be fair. 'Well, it will, won't it?' she
said with a sigh.

Rob made a rude noise.

'I couldn't care less how the board of Challender's
operates,' he admitted. 'All I want to do is be the best
obstetrician in Perth.'

'I know,' said Jo sympathetically. 'And I really admire
you for it.'

Rob gave a mirthless laugh.

'You're the only one who does,' he replied. 'Everybody
else thinks I'm crazy not wanting to step into Tom's
shoes at Challender's, but obstetrics is the only career
I've ever wanted. And I'm really grateful to you for
pushing me into this job. I don't know how I can ever
repay you.'

'Think nothing of it,' insisted Jo graciously. 'And, as
for repaying me, whenever I want a baby in future I'll
come to you.'

Rob's sudden gust of incredulous laughter made her
think twice about what she had said. Colour rushed into
her cheeks.

'I didn't mean it like that!' she protested.

Rob framed her face in his hands and smiled warmly
at her.

'You're priceless, Jo!' he exclaimed. 'Don't ever
change, will you?'

'I don't think I could even if I wanted to,' groaned Jo.
'I always seem to put my foot in it. But at least it doesn't
seem to matter when there are only the two of us.

Somehow I always feel relaxed and comfortable with
you.'

'I feel relaxed and comfortable with you, too,' declared
Rob thoughtfully. 'And, speaking of relaxing, how about
coming sailing with me this weekend?'

Jo hesitated. 'I'd love to,' she agreed finally. 'On one
condition.'

'What's that?'

'No more cat-burglar kisses.'

Rob sighed.

'Yes, I guess you're right,' he admitted reluctantly.
'OK, Jo. If you'll let me show you around Perth I
promise not to kiss you.'

The month that followed was a strange time for Jo—
both joyful and immensely difficult. She and Rob had
some wonderful times together, skimming over the blue
waters of the Swan River under full sail, lazing on
gleaming white beaches beside the Indian Ocean, feed-
ing the black swans on Lake Monger, eating dinners in
luxurious restaurants and casual barbecue lunches with
Mary Lou Fowler and her family. And all the time they
were drawn closer together by their shared interest in
Rob's work and their concern for Tom.

As for Rob's promise, he kept it scrupulously. He
never kissed Jo again, but, although she should have
been grateful, she wasn't. Somehow she had expected
that if they didn't touch each other they would no longer
want to do so. Which was pure madness. Because when
Rob came in to breakfast in a towelling robe with his
hair still damp from the shower and his tanned chest
exposed Jo frequently felt an insane urge to reach out
and touch him. And several times, when she was lounging in a bikini on the patio overlooking the river, she felt
his gaze burning through her with a hungry intensity. In
theory Tom should have been a chaperon of sorts. But
Tom seemed to delight in deliberately throwing them
together and, in any case, he was often too sick to leave
his room.

The sad fact was that the old man was sinking fast.
He liked to sit in a summer-house overlooking the blue,
sunlit river, but even the short walk up the garden to the
house made him gasp agonisingly for breath. Each day
he seemed to spend a larger amount of time resting, and
he was troubled by a frequent cough. Only the prospect
of the lavish seventieth birthday party which he was
planning seemed to keep him going. There were times
when Jo found the strain of nursing him very severe.
Tom had hired a second nurse to help with the daylight
routine and give Jo some time off, but inevitably most of
the nocturnal care fell on her shoulders. Rob did all he
could to help, but he was frequently called out to deliver
babies in the middle of the night. Yet at least Jo had the
consolation of knowing that her work was genuinely
valued. Whenever she despaired of her impossible role
in the Challender household one look at Tom's blue-
lipped face would convince her that she had made the
right choice.

But if Jo found satisfaction in her work she found very
little in her private life. Inevitably her blossoming friend-
ship with Rob soon led to clashes with Miranda. Whenever the svelte brunette was not flying off to New York
or Tokyo negotiating business deals, she seemed to be
slinking around the house in Dalkeith. And she had an
in-built radar for the moments when Rob and Jo had
their heads together over an obstetrics textbook or a
punctured Lilo from the swimming pool. To Jo's chagrin
they seemed to be forever springing guiltily apart as
Miranda arrived. Yet if Jo secretly nursed the hope that
Rob would one day realise that he preferred her to
Miranda she was doomed to disappointment. Whenever
Rob was invited to a charity ball or a high-society lunch
it was always Miranda who accompanied him.

On one of these occasions Jo went to Mary Lou in
search of tea and sympathy. Realising that her friend
was on night duty at St Jude's and probably wouldn't
be awake until about three in the afternoon, Jo decided

to kill time by visiting the young miner, Ken Lewis, whom she had treated on her first day at Rainbow End. She found him in the spinal unit of a large Perth hospital, strapped into a special rotating bed. When she entered the ward the bed was upside-down with Ken lying on his stomach looking down at a racing form guide on the floor. Although he couldn't see her face he was in good spirits, and full of praise for the way she and Rob had rescued him.

'They say I'll be walking as good as new in a few weeks,' he said with relief. 'And if it hadn't been for you and Doc Challender I reckon I'd be tied to a flamin' bed for the rest of me life. What can a bloke say about somethin' like that? I dunno how to tell you what I feel, but if I live to be ninety I'll never forget either of yez.'

Jo left the hospital walking on air. It was one of those moments of supreme satisfaction that compensated a hundredfold for the hardships of nursing. All the same, the euphoria didn't last long. By the time she reached Mary Lou's house she had slipped back into the depression that dogged her whenever she thought of Rob and Miranda and her own future. Sighing, she rang the doorbell and thought how lucky her friend was to be happily married. Mary Lou opened the door with her mouth full of pins.

'Hmm. I'd better not smile, you might have a medical emergency to deal with,' she commented, spitting them into her palm. 'How nice to see you, Jo! Is Rob with you?'

'No,' said Jo flatly.

'Oh, dear. Like that, is it?' replied Mary Lou. 'Come on in, I'll put the coffee on.'

Jo followed her into the sunny family room at the rear of the house. Mary Lou had a sewing cabinet set up in the middle of the room, a cutting board out on the floor, and a large, glossy fashion magazine pinned open on a noticeboard. There was a black and white cat batting an empty cotton-reel around the floor and a smell of freshly baked chocolate-chip cookies in the air.

'Oh, you are lucky to have a proper home!' commented Jo mournfully. 'Where are the kids?'

'At my mother's. Kids and sewing don't mix. Neither do cats, actually. Outside, Sheba.'

Shooing the cat out the back door, she fixed Jo with a penetrating look.

'Well, what's the trouble?' she demanded.

Jo sat down with a sigh, and flung her jacket carelessly over the back of the couch. 'I'm fed up!' she said through her teeth.

'Ah,' murmured Mary Lou acutely. 'Romantic troubles with Rob, I suppose?'

Jo gave her a startled glance. 'Is it that obvious?' she demanded.

Mary Lou grinned. 'Only to the trained observer,' she murmured soothingly. 'Mind you, I don't blame you. He's really quite a hunk. And anyone can see he's crazy about you.'

Jo spluttered.

'Don't be ridiculous!' she retorted. 'He's only got eyes for one woman. And that's Miranda Sinclair. You know, that woman lawyer I pointed out to you on television one night.'

'Oh, is that so?' queried Mary Lou with her eyebrows arched. 'Then why was he devouring you with his eyes last time you came here to visit?'

Jo blushed. 'He wasn't!' she protested. But she looked pleased.

'So you've really fallen for him in a big way, have you?' quizzed Mary Lou.

Jo nodded miserably.

'Although I don't know why I bother,' she complained. 'After all, I'm just not in the race. Miranda Sinclair is about thirty pounds lighter than I am, a thousand times more glamorous, and much more intelligent. She's always flying off to New York or being

interviewed about her views on the economy. She even
knows all about gold mines and the stock market. I'm so
dumb I thought a bull market was somewhere that you
sold cattle!'

'Oh, isn't it?' said Mary Lou blankly. 'Anyway, never
mind about all that rubbish, Jo. Rob didn't seem all that
interested in gold mines to me, and I don't believe men
really like skinny women much. Or, if they do, I'm going
to have to stop making chocolate-chip cookies! No, the
trouble is Rob takes you for granted. He probably
doesn't even realise how much he needs you, because
you're always there. What you've got to do is get him to
see you in a different light.'

Jo looked interested, but wary.

'Yes, but how?' she protested.

'Well, get dressed up, go somewhere glamorous. Let
him see that other men find you attractive too. There
must be a really posh party or something you could go
to, isn't there?'

Jo tapped her teeth thoughtfully with her thumbnail.

'Actually, Tom's having a real extravaganza for his
seventieth birthday,' she said slowly. 'No expense
spared. Oxen roasted on spits, a brass band, Bollinger
by the gallon, and every single inhabitant of Millionaires'
Row dancing the night away, not to mention all the
other beautiful people that are flying in from Melbourne
and Sydney for it.'

'Perfect!' cried Mary Lou enthusiastically. 'Then all
you need to do is get dressed to kill and make sure you
dance with every good-looking male in sight. Rob'll be
so jealous he'll probably drag you off by the hair and
propose to you on the spot.'

Jo giggled.

'I should be so lucky!' she exclaimed. 'No, it's a nice
idea, Mary Lou, but it just wouldn't work. The sort of
women who'll be there will have Givenchy dresses and
ropes of diamonds. What could I possibly wear that
would compare with that?'

Mary Lou darted across to the noticeboard, and unpinned the *Vogue* magazine. She flicked through until she came to a page with a stunning gold sheath evening dress with slits up to the knees and a swooping neckline.

'How about this?' she suggested, holding it up for Jo to see.

'Oh, sure,' said Jo tartly, peering at the fine print. 'I'd look great in that. Now all I need is the two thousand dollars to buy it.'

'I could make it for you,' asserted Mary Lou.

Their eyes met. Jo hesitated.

'I'd look ridiculous,' she protested. 'It has no shoulders at all. There must be magnets or something holding it up.'

'You'd look fabulous,' insisted Mary Lou.

'Could you really make it?' asked Jo.

'No worries,' stated Mary Lou airily.

'But it would take ages. How could I ever pay you for it?'

'Five thousand hours of babysitting would do for starters,' suggested Mary Lou impishly.

A wistful look crept over Jo's face.

'It would still be useless,' she said softly. 'I could never compete with Miranda Sinclair.'

'Of course you could!' protested Mary Lou. 'Don't be so chicken-hearted. Anyway, it's practically a criminal offence to let a nasty piece of work like Miranda get her claws into a man as nice as Rob. You mustn't surrender without a fight. You owe it to him to save him from himself.'

'Do you really think so?' asked Jo.

'Yes, I do,' said Mary Lou firmly. 'Well, what's it going to be? Surrender or war?'

A slow grin spread over Jo's face. 'War,' she said.

'Tom, are you sure you're well enough to go to this party?' asked Jo in a worried voice.

The old man lay back on his pillows, gasping feebly.

His face looked ashen and his lips were tinged with blue, but he pointed gamely at his mouth, where an Anginine tablet was dissolving, and motioned to Jo to wait for him. She felt his pulse and found it rapid and thready.

'I think I should call Rob,' she fretted.

With immense effort Tom shook his head. There was silence as he waited for the medication to take effect. Then slowly a tinge of colour washed back into his cheeks.

'No,' he whispered fiercely.

Knowing his stubborn nature, Jo shook her head and handed him another tablet, which he tucked under his tongue. Then she checked his blood pressure.

'A hundred and eighty-five over a hundred and ten,' she scolded. 'Honestly, Tom, this is absurd. You're really not fit for this party. You could kill yourself.'

A ghost of a smile flickered over Tom's blue lips.

'Then at least I'll go out with a bang,' he said with satisfaction. 'And there'll be plenty of doctors there, don't you worry, and most of them cardiologists. Gavin Lyall, Ron Simpson, Alistair McKendrick. In fact I feel sorry for any other poor bugger that has a heart attack in Perth tonight. They'll have to come here if they want to get treated!'

Jo smiled wryly and patted Tom on the hand.

'You're an old rogue,' she chided affectionately. 'Well, if I can't persuade you to give up the party, at least you should rest for a few minutes. The guests will be here soon.'

To her relief Tom closed his eyes, and soon his quiet breathing told her that he had slipped into sleep. Unfortunately he was clutching her hand as he dozed off, and Jo was reluctant to disturb him by moving it. Soon she began to get cramp in her back from bending over, and she had to slide down into a crouching position to ease it. She was still kneeling uncomfortably beside the bed when there was a firm knock at the door.

'Come in,' she whispered.

Rob put his head around the door and, seeing that Tom was asleep, crept in silently. He was dressed in a black dinner-jacket and black trousers that showed off his broad shoulders and muscular thighs. With his raven dark hair, cornflower-blue eyes and perfect white teeth he looked devastatingly handsome. It was no wonder that Jo suddenly felt miserably conscious of the simplicity of her white uniform and navy cardigan.

'What are you doing down there?' he demanded in exasperation.

'Tom fell asleep holding my hand, and I didn't want to disturb him,' she explained in a stage whisper. 'Can you help me up? My feet have got pins and needles now.'

Rob's strong, warm hand hauled her unceremoniously to her feet, but the movement woke Tom.

'Eh? What's going on?' he asked, sitting up.

'Your party, that's what!' replied Rob impatiently. 'Are you fit to come down or not? The guests will be here any minute.'

Jo opened her mouth to voice her fears, caught Tom's warning look, and remained silent.

'Of course I am! Fit as a fiddle!' insisted Tom. 'And dressed to kill, what's more. Now, you just give me an arm down them stairs, Bob, and she'll be apples!'

Rob exchanged a long, suffering look with Jo.

'How about you?' he asked with a hint of anxiety. 'Aren't you going to join the party?'

'Yes, I'll just have to run and change,' said Jo in a flustered voice.

As she spoke the musical peal of the doorbell sounded below.

'Go on,' she urged. 'I'll be down in a minute.'

But it took Jo a good fifteen minutes to shower, change into her glamorous new dress, and apply the make-up that Mary Lou had insisted was essential to complete the image. When she finally emerged from her bedroom and walked along to the landing above the hall she could hear that the brass band was already playing 'Happy Birthday'. Not wanting to interrupt Tom's big moment, she waited until the music, the cheers and the laughter had all died down before she made her entrance. But if Jo had expected to slip in unnoticed she had completely underestimated the impact she would make.

As she came slowly down the curving staircase one or two heads turned and a young blond man with the shoulders of a surfer let out a low whistle of appreciation. That was the signal for everybody else to look up. If Jo was embarrasssed she gave no sign of it. Defiantly she lifted her head, tossed back her long tawny-brown curls, and smiled. Tall and statuesque with perfect teeth, vivid amber eyes and a dazzling gold evening dress that revealed her creamy shoulders and high, full breasts, she looked magnificent. The young surfer was not the only man present who was impressed. As Jo swept gracefully down the marble staircase with one hand resting on the polished banisters, a low buzz of admiration broke out below her. But none of it meant as much to her as the silent, startled glance of the raven-haired man who stood apart from the rest of the crowd.

'Jo, you look superb!' exclaimed Rob, threading his way through the crowd to meet her.

'Doesn't she ever?' cut in a second baritone. 'My name's Scott Baintree, Jo, and I'm delighted to meet you.'

Jo looked slightly bemused as the tall, blond surfer pushed his way between her and Rob and shook her hand warmly. He had a pleasant, open face, but there was a wicked twinkle in his grey eyes.

'In fact, I'm so delighted to meet you,' he continued, 'that I'm hoping you'll let me get you a drink so that I can find out more about you.'

Jo was on the point of refusing when she caught Rob's stormy look, and recalled Mary Lou's advice. So she smiled dazzlingly.

'Why not?' she agreed.

After that the evening went with a swing. Scott
Baintree proved to be an amusing and likeable companion. He confessed that he came from the Baintree
Baked Beans family, but begged her not to hold it
against him, and spent the next four hours making
himself agreeable to her. Fetching her tall glasses of
champagne and plates of smoked salmon in aspic,
whirling her round the dance-floor and introducing her
to a crowd of riotous young people who kept spilling out
into the garden for scavenger-hunts and other lively
party-games. Whenever Rob attempted to approach Jo
she was always in the thick of a laughing, milling group
of young men, so that in the end he gave up. But as the
evening wore on Jo became more and more conscious of
his narrowed blue eyes following her wherever she went.
Even when he was on the dance-floor partnering
Miranda his gaze remained fixed on Jo as she pirouetted
by in Scott's embrace. But it was not until the band
struck up a tango shortly after midnight that matters
really came to a head.

Jo was not normally the sort of girl to be the life of the
party, but by now she had drunk several glasses of
Bollinger, and the bubbles seemed to be mounting to her
brain. And, while Scott Baintree might be an outrageous
flirt, he was also an exceptionally fine dancer. So that
when the impetuous, fiery chords of the tango sounded
through the ballroom Jo did not even hesitate. As Scott
pulled her imperiously on to the dance-floor her whole
body felt as if it were floating, and she let herself go in
time to the sensuous rhythm of his movements. Together
they dipped and plunged across the room with a fire and
precision that brought applause from some of the
bystanders. One by one the other couples came to a
standstill until at last only Scott and Jo were left on the
floor. For a couple of dizzying minutes they danced like
a pair of inspired gold medallists, charging, halting,
jerking their heads in perfect unison, and then changing
direction for another fiery manoeuvre. Out of the corner

of her eye Jo caught a glimpse of Rob scowling thunderously with Miranda clinging jealously to his arm. Then somebody flung a red rose into the air. Scott fielded it deftly and set it between Jo's teeth without even missing a beat. Silently breathing her thanks that there were no thorns in the stem, Jo smiled brilliantly and flung back her head. But just at that moment another pair of arms seemed to come from nowhere and encircle her waist.

'I think it's time somebody else enjoyed your dancing,' said Rob in a steely voice. 'Stand aside, Baintree.'

Scott gave him a swift, challenging look that was full of resentment. But whatever he saw in Rob's tense, determined face evidently made him think better of the challenge. He shrugged.

'Just as you like,' he replied lazily, and backed away to the sidelines.

A ripple of speculation went through the onlookers. But Rob either didn't notice or didn't care. If Scott had danced brilliantly, Rob danced like a man inspired. His powerful arms propelled Jo around the floor with an energy and fire she had never seen in him before. And, at the moment when their heads jerked to confront each other, she saw that his blue eyes were smouldering with a rage or passion that threatened to devour her. Nor was she the only person to notice it. With a brittle trill of laughter Miranda seized her old friend Stephen Lester by the arm, and dragged him on to the floor.

'Come on, Steve!' she commanded. 'Why should Rob and Jo have all the fun?'

Miranda's dancing was just as flamboyant as Rob's, but it was totally wasted on him. As he flashed around the floor he had eyes for nobody but Jo. Which would have been fine, except that his gaze was jealous and accusing and everybody, including Jo, noticed it. Her initial rush of exhilaration changed to an overwhelming sense of embarrassment and dismay. The red rose dropped to the floor and was crushed underfoot in their headlong march, as Jo glanced nervously at the by-standers. Her lapse of concentration made her stumble, and Rob caught her against him with fingers like steel.

'What's the matter?' he hissed. 'You looked as if you were ready to dance all night with Scott.'

Tears started to Jo's eyes. 'I'm tired,' she lied.

'Then why don't you go and have a rest?' suggested Miranda sweetly, coming to a halt beside them. 'Tom's sure to be needing you. And Rob and I will dance.'

She laid one slender, red-nailed hand on Rob's shoulder, but he shook it off. As he looked at her exquisite face with its calculating dark eyes his mouth hardened.

'I don't think so, Miranda,' he said clearly, with a contemptuous look at Stephen Lester. 'It seems to me you've already found a man who likes dancing to your tune. Come on, Jo. If you're tired we'll sit this one out on the terrace.'

And, before everyone's astonished eyes, he put one hand under Jo's arm and propelled her ruthlessly towards the French doors. As they reached the edge of the room Jo saw Tom's pale face turned towards them. His lips were bluish and his breathing was slightly laboured, but his blue eyes were as shrewd and thoughtful as ever.

'Tom——' she began, as they stumbled past him.

'Go on, love,' Tom urged her. 'I'll be fine, and it looks like Bob has things he wants to say to you.

The moment they were out of earshot of the ballroom Jo dragged her arm out of Rob's grasp and turned on him furiously.

'How could you?' she demanded angrily. 'You humiliated me in front of everyone, making a scene like that!'

'Did I?' retorted Rob in a hard voice. 'How odd! I thought after that exhibition with Scott Baintree that you rather enjoyed scenes. You were dancing like a Brazilian harlot!'

'How dare you?' flared Jo. 'Scott Baintree invited me

to dance in a perfectly courteous manner, and I accepted. There was nothing more to it. He didn't drag me off like some overbearing caveman the way you did!'

Rob laughed cynically.

'No, Baintree wouldn't!' he agreed. 'He's a bit more suave than that about getting what he wants, but he'll let you down in the finish, sweetie. His intentions are never serious.'

'Oh, and yours are, I suppose?' taunted Jo.

'I'll show you how serious my intentions are!' grated Rob.

And with a sudden deft movement he swept her into his arms, forced back her head and kissed her as she had never been kissed in her life before. Stars swung overhead, she felt the cold pressure of the stone balustrade against her back and smelled the overpowering scent of the white starry jasmine in the tub beside her. And, above all, she felt the warm, muscular hardness of Rob's body against hers, the demanding pressure of his mouth, the wild beating of his heart through the fabric of his dinner-jacket. Her lips opened softly and sweetly against his, and she let herself surrender to the waves of desire that were pulsing through her. Even when she heard hesitant footsteps come through the french doors, falter and then go back inside she did not so much as turn her head. But at last Rob released her, and she gazed helplessly up into his dark, brooding face.

'I love you, Jo,' he said harshly.

Her knees felt suddenly weak and shaky.

'What did you say?' she demanded through frozen lips.

'You heard me!' he retorted roughly.

There was a sudden burst of laughter near the french doors, and two or three couples spilt out on to the terrace. Rob seized her hand impatiently.

'We can't talk here,' he said. 'Come down to the summer-house.'

The summer-house was built into a leafy nook at the

very foot of the garden, so that only somebody familiar with the house would know it existed. Tom had had it fitted up as an auxiliary office, and often sat in it, talking into a dictaphone and watching the yachts sail by on the river. As they fought their way through the thick shrubs on the bank behind it Jo laid one hand on Rob's sleeve.

'It'll be locked,' she pointed out.

His only response was to hold up a key, which gleamed silver in the moonlight. Inserting it in the lock, he opened the door and dragged Jo in after him. Then he kicked the door shut, and tugged the string which controlled the bamboo blinds at the window. The moment the blinds fell with a crash down over the glass he took her in his arms. Kisses rained on her hair and eyelids and neck, and Rob's hands were doing wonderful things to her breasts and hips through the glossy fabric of her evening dress. Suddenly he slipped them down inside her strapless bodice and caressed the warm tips of her breasts. She let out a low groan and buried her face in his shoulder.

'I thought you wanted to talk,' she gasped.

'I did,' agreed Rob thickly. 'But this seemed like a better idea. Oh, Jo, I want you so badly. Just let me touch you, kiss you, bury my face in your beautiful, smooth skin.'

As he spoke he sank to his knees. His questing fingers found the zip to her dress, and suddenly the gleaming gold sheath slid in a crumpled heap on the floor. Another ruthless tug and her wisp of a bra followed suit. Then Rob buried his face exultantly in the tender fullness of her breasts. She felt his smooth hair tickle her nakedness and, threading her fingers through its silky, dark mass, she drew him closer to her. His warm mouth sought out her nipple, and she gave a small, choking whimper of delight as his tongue moved teasingly over the sensitive peak. Half-heartedly she tried to push him away, but he caught her hand in his strong fingers, and drew her naked body hard against him.

'No, let me touch you, Jo!' he begged urgently. 'I love you, I need you, I want you! You can't imagine how much I want you!'

There was no mention of marriage, but Jo was past caring. As Rob drew her down into his embrace she nestled against him, moulding her body to his, and hearing his ragged breathing with a delirious sense of triumph and delight. His hands tore frantically at the last scraps of her underwear, and then she was warm and naked in his arms.

'Touch me,' he breathed urgently. 'Help me undress. I want to feel your naked body against mine.'

Clumsily she fumbled with the unfamiliar buttons and fastenings. But soon he was naked beside her, the harsh planes and angles of his body gleaming in the crack of moonlight that spilt through the edge of the blind. Jo's hands explored the magnificent male power of his body with its taut, flat belly, the rough hair on the chest, the powerful, vigorous thighs. He groaned under her touch, and reached out to caress her.

'I wish I could see you properly,' she whispered.

'You will, sweetheart, you will,' he promised throatily. 'We're going to be doing a lot more of this. But for now we'll just have to find out way by touch.'

His arms came around her and she felt his breath stir her curly hair. With a deep sigh she closed her eyes and gave herself up to the intoxicating pleasure of his kisses moving down over her neck, her throat, her breasts, her belly. . . But just as she thought she would swoon with sheer pleasure a sudden imperious beeping noise made them both stop dead.

'What is it?' demanded Jo, scrambling to her feet.

Rob swore violently.

'Those bloody Stevenson twins, I suppose!' he exclaimed bitterly. 'Why on earth couldn't that woman have delivered tomorrow?'

He stumbled to his feet, groped for his jacket in the

darkness, and switched off the beeper. Then he began to haul on his clothes unceremoniously.

'I'd better get to a phone,' he said.

'There's a cordless one on the table there,' Jo reminded him. 'Tom often uses it here. You won't need to switch on the overhead light—the numbers light up automatically.'

While Rob punched in the digits she began slowly to get dressed herself.

'Nearing the end of the first stage, you say? And one is a posterior presentation? All right, I'm on my way,' promised Rob.

He paused and dropped a swift kiss on the top of Jo's head.

'I'm sorry about this,' he said sincerely. 'But maybe we can talk about it tomorrow. You know, sometimes I don't think any woman in her right mind would marry an obstetrician.'

And, with that, he was out the door. Left alone, Jo finished zipping her dress, hunted her shoes out of a dark corner, and sat down with a defeated sigh to put them on. What next? she wondered despairingly. And what did he mean by that last remark? Was he really thinking of asking her to marry him? Well, whatever the answer to that was, she really ought to get back to the party before she was missed. Combing her hair with her fingers, Jo rose to her feet and picked her way back towards the door. But as she reached it the sound of footsteps on the path outside made her freeze. Jo held her breath as Miranda's familiar nasal voice drifted clearly through the night air.

'Did you see what Rob looked like as he left, Steve?' she demanded. 'That little slut must have dragged him backwards through a hedge before she pulled him down underneath it. I really don't know why they don't give her her marching orders. It's exactly the same situation as Tom was in three years ago with that Norris woman who pretended she was a nurse, and then when she'd taken the old boy in she tried to get him to marry her. Rob soon put a stop to that, so then Norris decamped with all Bet's jewels. It was all hushed up, of course, and Rob's been very wary of fortune-hunters ever since. If you ask me, Jo was setting her line for Tom from the minute she met him, but now that she can see he's dying she's decided to pursue Rob instead. Luckily he's wise to her tricks. He told me himself that she's nothing but a greedy little gold-digger. Of course, that doesn't stop him amusing himself with her. Still, that's men, I suppose. Oh, look, Steve, they're starting the fireworks up on the bank. Shall we go and watch?'

The voices faded away, but Jo remained where she was, frozen with dismay. Miranda's words tumbled over and over in her tired brain, and she struggled to make sense of them. Tom and some fortune-hunter in the past. Bet's jewels. Jo setting her line. But in the end the only thing that stuck was that awful, contemptuous statement of Rob's. 'A greedy little gold-digger'. Was that really what he thought of her? Because, if it was, the only possible thing she could do was resign immediately. Making her way out on to the path in front of the summer-house, Jo gazed bitterly around her. The fireworks had stopped, and the party was obviously over. Blinded by tears, she made her way slowly up the garden. The evening which had begun so brightly was in ruins.

CHAPTER SEVEN

As SHE came in through the french doors she was met by the cardiologist Gavin Lyall, still resplendent in a black dinner-suit, but with a weary look on his face. In the background several people in the uniform of a catering firm were clearing away dirty glasses and emptying ashtrays, but the guests had obviously gone home.

'Ah, there you are, Nurse Webster,' said Dr Lyall with relief. 'I didn't like to leave until I found you. Tom's been asking for you.'

'Is he all right?' asked Jo with a sudden pang of anxiety.

'He's very short of breath, and the Captopril's not holding him. I wouldn't be surprised if he has to go into hospital pretty soon. I'd like you to double his Frusemide dosage, and see that he takes two tablets at lunchtime as well as in the morning. But I'll call again tomorrow and check on him.'

'All right. Thank you,' said Jo. 'I'll go straight up to him.'

'That's the girl. Don't bother seeing me out, I know my own way. Oh, if you'll excuse my mentioning it, Nurse, you might want to freshen up before you go in to him. There are some leaves in your hair.'

'Thanks,' murmured Jo distractedly.

She was past caring very much, but she did slip into her own bathroom and comb her hair before she went to see Tom. Her face in the mirror shocked her. All the vitality seemed to have drained out of it, and she looked pale and miserable. Even so, she managed to summon a bright smile before she tapped on Tom's door. But Tom wasn't fooled. Although he lay in bed looking weak and ill his eyes were as piercing as ever.

'What went wrong?' he demanded imperiously.

'W-what do you mean?' asked Jo.

'Don't beat around the bush, girl,' whispered Tom feebly. 'You know bloody well what I mean. I saw Bob kissin' you on the terrace, and he didn't take you down to the summer-house just to check your blood pressure. I thought he was gunna pop the question tonight. So what went wrong?'

A lump rose in Jo's throat.

'Everything,' she said in a choking voice.

Turning away to hide the tears that threatened to spill over at any moment, she stood with one fist pressed to her mouth.

'Come on, love,' wheedled the old man. 'You come and sit on the bed and tell old Tom all about it.'

'I can't,' wailed Jo. 'It's too humiliating.'

But she sat down on the bed, all the same.

'Course you can love,' coaxed Tom. 'You don't mean to tell me you're not in love with him, do you?'

'I was in love with him,' admitted Jo through trembling lips. 'But it's all spoilt now.'

'What's that young fool Bob said to upset you like this?' demanded Tom in an annoyed voice.

Jo cleared her throat. 'Well, he didn't actually say much at all,' she admitted. 'Not at first.'

Tom gave a wheezy chuckle.

'No, I suppose he wouldn't,' he conceded. 'But what happened afterwards? He must have done something wrong to get you in such a state.'

Jo flushed delicately. 'Well, it wasn't just Rob,' she said in a low, uneven voice. 'Actually, he was called away to deliver some babies, and then Miranda came by while I was still inside the summer-house. I overheard her talking to someone, and she said——'

She broke off, unable to continue. But Tom's black thatched eyebrows drew together fiercely.

'Go on,' he urged in a dangerous voice.

Jo cast him a wary glance.

'She said Rob thought I was a gold-digger and he was only amusing himself with me.'

'And you believed her?' Tom's voice was scathing.

'Why shouldn't I?' retorted Jo. 'She didn't know I was in the summer-house.'

Tom snorted sceptically.

'After what happened in the ballroom tonight I reckon she'd have known if you went to Greenland,' he said contemptuously. 'She probably had tracker-dogs out after you. No, I reckon she knew you was there all the time, love, and just said that stuff to upset you. Which it has done. But why did you take it all so serious? I thought you and Rob had decided a long time ago that all that nonsense about the car and the trip to Hawaii was just a good joke.'

Jo swallowed painfully.

'There was more to it than that,' she admitted.

Tom fixed her with a look that made her understand how he had carved an empire out for himself.

'Go on,' he insisted relentlessly.

'I can't,' whispered Jo. 'It's about you.'

Tom's lips set in a grim line. His thick arthritic fingers knotted slowly and painfully together, and his breath came in gasps.

'Well, if you won't say it I reckon I'll have to,' he panted. 'I reckon she said "That old fool Tom got took in once by a pretty woman that pretended she was a nurse, but was only after his money. Well, Jo's another one of the same sort. Except now she's found Tom won't marry her she's got her hooks into Bob instead." Is that about the size of it, love?'

Jo looked startled, and then slowly nodded.

'Well, don't you worry your pretty head about that,' urged Tom earnestly.

'You mean it's not true?' asked Jo with dawning relief.

Tom winced. 'Oh, it's true about the Norris woman,'

he said with a sigh. 'She took me to the cleaners good and proper after my Bet died, old fool that I was, and Bob had to step in and deliver her marching orders. Which is why he was so suspicious of you right at the start. But I never thought you was like that, Jo. And I'm damned sure Bob don't think so any more either. So don't you worry, love. We'll fix it up between us.'

Jo gave him a tormented look.

'I don't know, Tom,' she murmured. 'If Rob really thinks that about me, I'll have to do something. I can't go on as we are.'

'Do what?' asked Tom uneasily.

Jo took a long, ragged breath.

'I'll have to resign,' she said. 'Oh, Tom, don't you see? I can't go on living in the same house with Rob if he really thinks I'm just a fortune-hunter.'

Tom's distress was obvious. His hands clenched and unclenched, and his wrinkled face worked violently.

'Hand me them tablets,' he ordered.

Jo watched in dismay as he shook an Anginine tablet into his palm and placed it under his tongue. For a couple of minutes he lay with his eyes closed and his breath coming in shallow gasps. Then at last he opened his eyes and looked at her fiercely.

'Don't you leave yet, my girl,' he ordered. 'This is all my fault. And I'll fix things up, I promise yer.'

In spite of her late night Jo woke the next morning at her usual time of six o'clock. As soon as she was dressed she slipped along the upstairs corridor to Tom's bedroom. On the way she passed Rob's door, which was shut fast. She felt her heartbeat speed up as she tiptoed by. I wish I was in there with him, she thought. Oh, please, Tom, work some kind of miracle and make this all come right! But when she entered Tom's room she saw that he was in no condition to work miracles. In fact he looked in need of a miracle himself. His face was pale with a bluish tinge around the lips, and he was gasping for breath. However, after Jo administered his Captopril and Frusemide tablets he slowly improved and, after she had given him his bath and breakfast, she left him to read the financial papers while she went downstairs to get something to eat herself.

Shortly after ten o'clock Jo was in the dining-room flicking sightlessly through a magazine when Rob strode in. He was casually dressed in navy corduroy trousers and a navy windcheater, and her heart quickened at the sight of him. Nervously she scanned his face for any sign of contempt or derision, but he simply gave her a lazy smile. His blue eyes and engaging grin looked heart-breakingly familiar and completely innocent.

'What's wrong?' he asked, sensing her tension.

'Nothing,' replied Jo hastily, glancing down at her magazine.

He came round the table and his warm hands descended on her shoulders. Burying his face in her tumbled curls, he nuzzled the back of her neck. 'Gold-digger', a malicious voice whispered inside her head. Her entire body stiffened.

'Don't,' she begged in a low, taut voice.

'Something *is* wrong, isn't it?' demanded Rob with genuine concern.

He pulled out one of the Hepplewhite chairs, and sat down beside her. Then he laid one hand on her knee. She flinched at the contact, feeling currents of desire flare through her, followed immediately by a tidal wave of suspicion and resentment. His face was so close that she could see the dark fringe of his eyelashes against his cornflower-blue eyes and the faint shadow of his beard underneath his skin.

'You're not regretting what happened last night, are you?' he demanded in that low, husky voice that made her quiver with longing.

'Not exactly,' she murmured in stifled tones.

'Then what——?' he began.

He was interrupted by the arrival of the housekeeper with fresh coffee, eggs, bacon and toast.

'Thanks, Mrs Lawson,' said Rob, taking his hand off Jo's knee and loading up his plate. 'Aren't you eating, Jo?'

'Not hungry,' replied Jo in a small voice.

When the housekeeper had left Rob fixed Jo with a quizzical look.

'What's the matter?' he demanded. 'You're as jumpy as a cat on hot bricks.'

'How did the delivery go last night?' asked Jo, desperately trying to change the subject.

'Oh, great,' replied Rob enthusiastically. 'I had to deliver one with forceps, but the other birth was completely straightforward. They were both over three kilos, and they're doing fine. Their mother is thrilled to bits with them.'

They had just finished discussing the high incidence of forceps deliveries in Australia and what could be done to prevent it, when there was another knock at the dining-room door.

'Come in,' called Rob.

This time a small, grey-haired man in a pin-striped suit came respectfully into the room.

'Good morning, Dr Challender,' he said courteously, holding out his hand. 'I don't know if you remember me. My name is Reynolds, Frank Reynolds. I'm one of your uncle's solicitors. He called me in urgently this morning because he wanted to make some changes to his will.'

'His will?' echoed Rob anxiously. 'Has his condition got worse during the night?'

'No, no, no,' Mr Reynolds assured him soothingly. 'Please sit down, Dr Challender and finish your breakfast. No, I merely came in to tell you that Mr Challender would like to see you and Nurse Webster in his study as soon as it's convenient for you both. I believe he has in mind some redistribution of his assets which he wishes to discuss with you.'

Mr Reynolds bowed and withdrew, leaving Rob and Jo staring at each other in bewilderment.

'Do you know what this is about?' demanded Rob.

'Not a clue,' replied Jo.

Yet there was a tremor in her voice as she recalled her last night's conversation with Tom. The old man had promised to fix everything, but what on earth was he up to now? Rob gave her a suspicious glance, and gulped down his coffee.

'Well, let's go and find out,' he said curtly.

Tom was sitting behind the huge mahogany desk in his study when Rob and Jo entered. His breathing was shallow and difficult, but there was a determined look on his face. There was no sign of Mr Reynolds in the room.

'All right,' said Tom. 'Sit down, both of yez. What I'm about to say may come as a bit of a shock to yez, but I don't believe in beatin' around the bush, so I'll give it to you straight. Bob, I want you to marry Jo.'

Jo had never heard such a profound silence since the days she'd attended the New South Wales high diving championships. Stunned, she took a swift breath and held it. The silence seemed to roar in her ears like the prelude to the bursting of some gigantic dam. And then it came.

'Oh, do you?' queried Rob softly.

He sat forward in his chair and stared Tom directly in the eye. But Tom stood his ground and matched him stare for stare.

'Yes, I do,' he replied tranquilly.

'You don't think, by any chance, that I might want to make my own matrimonial arrangements?' demanded Rob, still in that same velvety, menacing undertone.

Tom stroked his wrinkled chin thoughtfully.

'Could be,' he said reasonably. 'But I can't see that

you're havin' much bloody success so far. You bin
messin' about with that Miranda woman for near on
three years and you still can't see through her. Then a
nice girl like Jo comes along, just right for yer, and
you're too flamin' stupid to see it. So I thought I'd better
hurry things along a bit.'

'Oh, did you just?' growled Rob. 'Well, let me tell
you, you can keep your interfering nose out of my affairs!
I'll marry whom and when I please, and I won't ask
your advice when I do!'

Tom pressed his fingers into a spire and gazed serenely
at the ceiling.

'You know,' he said conversationally, 'That's pretty
well word for word what I said to you in this very room
three years ago. Back when that Norris piece was after
me. I didn't thank you for interferin' at the time, but
I'm ready to admit now that you done the right thing.
What I needed then was a swift kick in the pants, and
you gave it to me, Bob. Well, now I'm returnin' the
compliment.'

Rob shot his uncle a resentful look.

'I can do without your compliments,' he said sourly.
'And why the hell are you so keen to push me into
marriage anyway?'

Tom smiled wistfully.

'Cause I'm runnin' out of time, lad,' he replied. 'I've
got a fancy to see you wed and settled down before I
turn up me toes, and that don't give me much time to
pussyfoot around. I'll make it worth yer while, you
know. Both of yez.'

'What's that supposed to mean?' asked Rob in a
dangerous voice.

Tom beamed. He looked so much like a small, wizened
Father Christmas that Jo fully expected him to sling a
sack across the desk and cry 'Ho! Ho! Ho!'

'Half a million dollars each, cash on the nail, the day
you tie the knot,' he promised. 'Can't say fairer than
that!'

Jo half rose to her feet, and then sank back in her chair with a gasp of astonishment and dismay. Half a million dollars! It was a trifling sum to Tom, but it would certainly buy Rob a nice obstetrics practice. All the same, Tom must be mad if he thought his nephew would rise to the bait. Rob will be furious, she thought, bracing herself for the outcry. Absolutely furious. Rob was.

'God Almighty!' he roared, springing to his feet and slamming one powerful palm down on the desk. 'Have you been trading in commodities so long that you think everything in the world can be bought and sold, provided the price is right? I thought you had some ethics, Tom Challender, but it seems I was wrong! You're nothing but a power-hungry, pig-headed, interfering old fool, and I'll thank you to keep out of my affairs from now on.'

Seeing Tom flinch at this violent speech, Jo tugged at Rob's sleeve.

'Don't shout at him!' she begged. 'He meant well.'

Rob rounded on her.

'And you can damned well stay out of it, too!' he exclaimed. 'Although I suppose you're the one who put him up to it. I should have listened to Miranda last night! She tried to tell me you were only after me for the Challender money, but I was fool enough to think you really cared about me. Well, I can see how ridiculous that idea was now. You were never interested in anything but the size of Challender's balance sheet, were you?'

'You've got a nerve!' cried Jo. 'I'm not after your money, and I never was. And, as for accusing Tom of thinking everyone's for sale, how about you? The first time I ever met you you tried to buy me off with a roll of banknotes!'

Rob laughed mirthlessly.

'What was the problem? Wasn't it large enough?' he taunted.

Jo drew in a swift, sharp breath and slapped his face.

'How dare you?' she gasped.

There was a sudden choking groan from behind the desk. Rob turned and let out an anxious shout.

'Tom!'

The old man was slumped forwards against the desk with one hand pressed to his chest. Rob flew around the desk and hauled him back into his chair. Jo clapped her hands guiltily to her mouth, and then ran for the telephone. But, as Tom flopped into place like a rag-doll, he looked over Rob's powerful shoulder, opened one eye and gave her an unmistakable wink.

'Aren't you going to call an ambulance?' demanded Rob savagely. 'Don't you care what happens to him?'

Torn between exasperation and amusement, Jo sat back in her own chair. Her heart was still pounding violently from the after-effects of the quarrel and Tom's collapse, but she now felt an overwhelming urge to burst out laughing. Or crying.

'He's faking, Rob,' she said in the steadiest voice she could manage. 'Financial blackmail didn't work, so now he's trying the emotional kind.'

Rob's jaw hardened, and he looked intently down at Tom's contorted face.

'Is this true?' he demanded bitterly.

Tom's eyes fluttered open. His face relaxed.

'I do feel a lot better now,' he said apolgetically.

Rob gave an exasperated sigh, and strode across the room.

'Well, in that case I'll leave you two to get on with rewriting the will and carving up the empire,' he said contemptuously. 'I was up half the night, and I could do with some rest!'

The door slammed behind him, leaving the pictures on the walls swinging violently. Tom looked ruefully at Jo.

'Do you think I put me foot in it, love?' he asked innocently.

Jo winced. 'Oh, Tom!' she wailed. 'Of course you did!'

'Don't worry, Jo,' he pleaded. 'He'll come round. It's just that he's so flamin' obstinate—I can't think where he gets it from. But he'll soon realise that he's barkin' up the wrong tree by blamin' you. Don't you reckon, love?'

Jo wasn't so sure. The angry glint in Rob's blue eyes and the dangerous set of his jaw hadn't seemed very encouraging to her. But Tom's gaze was so guilty and pleading that she didn't have the heart to disillusion him.

'Yes, I suppose you're right,' she agreed wearily.

'Then you won't leave just yet, will yer, love?' he insisted.

'Look, Tom, I——' began Jo.

But just at that moment the telephone rang.

'Hello. Challender's,' said Tom. 'He's what? Old Clarrie? Gawd, I don't believe it! A gold nugget, you say? How big? Cripes! That's a turn up for the books, if it's true. Out along the Cutler's Springs Road, you say? No, I reckon that's his claim fair and square, and good luck to him! You bet I'll be out there, mate, on the first plane I can get. Wild horses wouldn't keep me away! And tell the old bugger I want to be the first to shout him a beer. Cheers, mate!'

Tom hung up the receiver, and a slow grin spread over his leathery face.

'Well, if that don't beat everything!' he breathed. 'That was Ted Fisher from the assay office in Rainbow End. He reckons Old Clarrie has found a gold nugget the size of an emu's egg out alongside the Cutler's Springs Road. By gum, who'd have thought it, eh? Anyway, Clarrie wants me to come out and check that it's genuine and his lease is in order and everythin'. He don't trust nobody else. Well, I'd better get crackin'. I've got a lot to do if I want to get to Rainbow End before nightfall. I'll need a chartered aircraft, a lawyer that knows the leases well, a jeep to collect me at the other end——'

'Tom, you're not serious?' cut in Jo. 'You can't really be planning to fly back to Rainbow End? The trip could kill you!'

But Tom simply brushed aside her objections.

'Don't you worry, love,' he said cheerfully, as he reached for the telephone. 'Gavin Lyall will be over in half an hour. He'll tell you I'm fit to go. Anyway, I'll bloody well walk if he doesn't!'

To Jo's astonishment Gavin Lyall did agree to let Tom make the trip. Not that he actually said he was fit for it, but it was clear that nothing would stop him.

Consequently, at two o'clock in the afternoon Jo found herself at Perth Airport ready to board a Piper Navajo light aircraft. The flight promised to be just as nerve-racking as her first journey with Tom. Rob Challender was treating her to the same scowling glances as before, and his conversation was limited to curt requests about the oxygen cylinder and Tom's medication. As for Tom, even the drive from Dalkeith seemed to have exhausted him, and he lay on his stretcher-bed with his eyes closed and his breath coming in rapid, shallow gasps. He'll be lucky if he lasts the journey, thought Jo with a tremor of anxiety. The same thought must have occurred to Rob, for he crouched beside the old man with an expression of surprising tenderness on his rugged face, and gripped the frail, gnarled hand.

'Anything I can get you before take-off, mate?' he asked.

With a great effort Tom's eyelids fluttered open.

'Can't go yet,' he whispered. 'Gotta wait for the lawyer. Want to make sure Clarrie's claim is safe.'

Just then a blur of movement on the tarmac caught Jo's attention. To her dismay she looked out and saw the sleek, dark head of Miranda Sinclair drawing along-side the plane. She was riding in an airport buggy and, as it came to a halt, she hopped smartly out, gave her already faultless hair a swift pat, and climbed nimbly aboard the plane. As always, she looked as if she had stepped out of a fashion magazine. What the well-dressed corporate raider is wearing, thought Jo sourly. Houndstooth suit, elegant cream blouse, black Italian shoes and a leather attaché case that would pay the national debt off.

'So sorry I'm late,' she apologised charmingly. 'I was in court until the very last moment.'

'Oh, my Gawd,' murmured Tom feebly, rolling his eyes. 'Not you!'

Miranda eased herself gracefully past him, and came to halt beside Rob, who was still crouching next to the bed. She dropped a swift kiss on his cheek.

'Hello, darling,' she greeted him, ruffling his thick black hair. 'How nice to see you again.'

Rob's eyes kindled and he smiled warmly at her. Tom gave him a pained look.

'All that glisters isn't gold, mate,' he told Rob. 'And don't you forget it!'

Miranda's smile froze on her face.

'What's the matter with him?' she asked bluntly. 'Is his mind wandering?'

Rob's mouth tightened and the warmth vanished from his eyes, but he said nothing. Climbing into his seat, he snapped the belt-buckle shut and sat upright for take-off., Miranda sat beside him, and in a couple of minutes they were airborne. Tom had to have oxygen during the flight, and Jo secretly hoped that he would call off the whole expedition, but pure stubbornness seemed to keep him going.

At the Rainbow End airport they were met by Ted Fisher, a big suntanned man in a wide-brimmed hat. Jo had rung ahead to organise a wheelchair for Tom, and Ted strode out on to the tarmac pushing it ahead of him as easily as if it were a child's toy. He shook hands warmly with the Challenders and Jo, but gave Miranda a wary nod.

'G'day, Tom. Bob. How ya goin', Jo? Afternoon, Miss Sinclair.'

'Good afternoon,' replied Miranda briskly. 'Have you got some transport organised for us?'

'Yeah, too right. Round in the car park. Just follow me.'

Pushing Tom effortlessly in front of him, he led the way to a battered jeep, coated with red dust. Miranda looked horrified.

'Couldn't you have found something more comfortable?' she demanded. 'After all, with Tom in the condition he is, he won't want to be jolted around.'

'Oh, come on, Miranda,' said Rob impatiently. 'It's only a mile to the assay office. Tom should be right for that distance.'

'Yeah, well that's just it, though,' admitted Ted unhappily, pushing his hat back on his head and scratching his bald forehead. 'The nugget's not at the assay office.'

'Well, where is it, then?' demanded Rob in a startled voice.

'Out at Clarrie's camp, along the Cutler's Springs Road. Along with Old Clarrie himself. Well, you know what the old geezer's like, Rob. When he made his find he was out in the middle of nowhere with that old mule of his, and he reckoned she wasn't up to riding into town. Besides, he didn't want to leave the gold for fear somebody would jump his claim. So he flagged down a passing car and asked them to deliver a letter to me explaining it all.'

Ted fished a filthy, crumpled sheet of paper out of his back-pocket, and waved it in the air. It was covered with the sort of huge, straggling print that a six-year-old would have done.

'Anyway,' he continued, 'in the letter Clarrie asked me to contact Tom and tell him what had happened. He reckoned Tom was the one bloke he could trust to see that he didn't get diddled out of his find, so he wanted me to bring Tom out to his camp to sort everything out.'

'But how do we know he really has discovered gold, if you haven't even seen the nugget?' demanded Miranda. 'Couldn't it all just be a tall story? Or couldn't he have simply found fool's gold? Iron pyrites or something like that?'

Ted shrugged.

'I don't reckon we'll know that until we get there,' he said, scratching his head again.

But Tom snorted contemptuously.

'Fool's gold!' he sniffed. 'Old Clarrie wouldn't make a mistake like that. If he says it's gold, then it's gold! Now are we gunna stand here yakkin' all day or are we gunna get movin'?'

'Are you sure you're up to a trip over rough roads like that?' asked Rob in a troubled voice.

'Course I am!' agreed Tom eagerly. 'Mind you, I'd better have you and Jo in the back with me in case I get took bad on the way.'

That disposed of Miranda's chances of sitting with Rob, thought Jo with a smile as she climbed into the back seat after Tom. But all the same, the old man could have spared himself the trouble. Instead of following Jo into the jeep Rob went round to the other side of the vehicle and climbed in so that Tom was wedged between them. An obscure ache spread through Jo's entire body. Only this morning he was kissing me in the dining-room, she thought, and now he can't even bear to sit beside me. Oh, Tom! What have you done to us?

As the red landscape flashed by with its blue upturned bowl of sky overhead, its grey saltbush and its flocks of raucous cockatoos wheeling and swooping among the eucalyptus trees, Jo stole an occasional swift glance at Rob. Once he was staring straight at her with a fierce, resentful expression that went straight to her heart. But every other time he was looking intently at Miranda, who sat in the front seat talking about mining leases and the company's rights.

At last they came around a bend and saw the dirty yellowish canvas of Clarrie's tent in the distance.

'There he is!' exclaimed Rob. 'Look. Over on the mullock heap.'

The jeep plunged off the road and came to a halt under a huge gum tree next to another vehicle. Gingerly they all clambered out, and they saw that Rob was right. Only a few yards away to one side of the grimy tent was a huge pile of rocks and red earth. And, on top of it, with his bristling beard thrust out and a large shotgun in his hands, sat Old Clarrie.

'G'day, mate!' panted Tom gleefully, advancing laboriously with his hand outstretched. 'So you finally done it, eh?'

Clarrie's suspicious face split into a wide grin, displaying pink gums and a sprinkling of yellow teeth.

'Too right, mate!' he agreed, laying down his shotgun and shaking hands. 'Take a look at this.'

He reached into an old khaki knapsack and reverently unwrapped a huge yellow nugget, as large as two doubled fists. Jo heard Miranda catch her breath, then Clarrie handed the nugget to Tom.

'Whadda ya reckon?' he asked casually.

Tom sat down breathlessly and took a small eyepiece out of his back-pocket, which he screwed into place in his right eye. Then he examined the nugget carefully. There was a profound silence as they all held their breath.

'I reckon you're a damned lucky man,' he said slowly.

Clarrie let out a whoop and almost tumbled back off the mullock heap. The two old men fell into each other's arms, and there was a great deal of back-slapping and yodelling, which left Tom gasping for breath and mopping his forehead. Miranda's lip curled, and she stepped gingerly forward over the rough red earth to inspect the nugget. But, as she bent to pick it up, Clarrie's shotgun barred her way.

'Nothin' personal,' he explained firmly. 'But I ain't gunna let nobody but Tom Challender touch that nugget.'

In the confused uproar that followed, with all its talk of mining leases and royalties and claims, Jo found herself in the background. She wandered across to the spot where Clemmie the mule stood tethered under a large, shady tree. Delving into her bag, Jo produced an apple and cut it up with her penknife. Then she held the pieces on the flat of her palm and watched as the animal greedily snuffled them up. She could not help thinking of the first time she and Rob had visited Clarrie's camp, and her lips curved into a nostalgic smile as she remembered the barbecued camel and the violin sonata. Glancing over the mule's back, she was startled to find Rob confronting her. Colour washed into her face.

'I-I didn't know you were there,' she murmured hesitantly. 'I was thinking of the first time we came here.'

'So was I,' rejoined Rob.

His face was grim, but some powerful emotion flared in his blue eyes.

'Listen, Jo——' he began.

But at that moment the discussion that was going on at the mullock heap reached a crescendo.

'No!' roared Tom Challender, slapping his leg. 'No, you damned well will not! Can't you get it through your head, woman, I brought you out here to see that Clarrie's interests were protected, not mine? And I'll be damned if I let you get away with this!'

'Rob. . .' murmured Jo.

'Not now, Jo!' retorted Rob curtly.

Shaking her off, he raced across the uneven red ground to the spot where Tom and Miranda were confronting each other. Tom's face was purple with rage and his slight frame was shaking. Miranda looked equally furious, and Jo felt a pang of dismay shoot through her as she saw Rob grip the other girl's shoulders and swing her round to face him. Her last shred of hope died in that instant. Obviously Miranda meant more to Rob than anybody in the world. Even Tom. So what chance did she have?

Defeated, she went back to the jeep and climbed inside. Let them settle it on their own. It was nothing to do with her. But two or three minutes later Tom and Clarrie appeared beside the vehicle. Jo wound down the window.

'What is it?' she asked wearily.

'Me and Clarrie want to ask you a favour,' said Tom. Carefully drawing in breath, he spoke in a loud, clear voice obviously intended to carry as far as possible. 'We reckon you're the only one we can trust.'

'What do you want me to do?' enquired Jo, feeling curious in spite of herself.

Tom produced a bundle wrapped in rags, and turned back one corner to display the precious gold metal below.

'We want you to take this here nugget in to Rainbow End and deposit it in my safe for the weekend until Clarrie can get it weighed and analysed at the assay office. Will you do that for us, love?'

This was spoken in the same ringing voice as before. Puzzled, Jo glanced around the camp-site and saw Rob and Miranda with their heads together under a tree, and then her brain cleared. Of course. Tom was giving her a chance to rehabilitate her character in Rob's eyes. Entrusting her with a nugget that was probably worth millions of dollars. Any self-respecting gold-digger would simply disappear into the sunset with it and never be seen again. Not that Rob seemed to care. He was still holding Miranda's arm and talking in a low, rapid voice as if nothing else in the world mattered to him. In fact he didn't even look round as Tom spoke.

'Yes, of course I will, Tom,' she agreed wearily.

'Although I think it's a waste of time. But what about the rest of you? Don't you want to come back to town?'

'Nope,' said Tom firmly. 'Better for you to do this on your own, love. Now listen carefully. I've writ down the combination of my safe here for you, but when you've locked the nugget away you burn the paper, won't you? We'll stick around here and look for more gold. You can come and get us later.'

'All right,' agreed Jo. 'Are you sure this suits you too, Clarrie?'

'Yep,' insisted Clarrie. 'Me and Clemmie trust yer, love.'

As she jolted off over the rough road Jo felt a sudden rush of warmth at the trust and affection the old men had shown her. But that was soon followed by a wave of bitterness. Why couldn't Rob show her the same trust as Tom? A lump rose in her throat as she remembered the times she and Rob had spent together. Good times and bad. Saving the young miner after the rock-fall, enduring the tragedy of a baby's death, quarrelling, laughing, sharing each other's lives. And then only last night coming together in a moonlit summer-house with a passion that had left her breathless and shaken. Surely, after all they had been through together, Rob couldn't still believe she was a fortune-hunter? Or could he?

Jo let out a long, sobbing breath. Well, whatever Rob believed, it was no longer her concern. Because it wasn't only a question of how Rob saw her as a human being, it was also a question of how he saw her as a woman. Deep down she had always known that Rob would have to make a choice between her and Miranda. And her final glimpse of Rob holding Miranda in his arms left Jo in no possible doubt about his choice. It was Miranda Sinclair, with all the glitter of the business world, who had really captured his heart. Not plain, ordinary Jo Webster.

Jo swallowed hard and lifted her chin. Well, it was

time she made some choices too, she resolved. And her first choice was quite clear. However long Tom Challender and the others waited, Jo would never return to Old Clarrie's camp.

CHAPTER EIGHT

IT WAS nearly dark when Jo reached Rainbow End. She drove straight to Tom's house and, squinting down at his scrawled figures, eventually deciphered the combination to the safe. Opening it up, she gazed inside. Listlessly she noted that there was a large stack of hundred-dollar notes on the central shelf. Probably seventy or eighty-thousand dollars, she thought without interest. Now if I were really a gold-digger I'd be in my seventh heaven. But since I'm not they can just stay there. Heaving the carefully wrapped nugget inside, she slammed the door with a clang and then checked to see that it was secure. After that she burned the paper in the sitting-room fireplace, and then wandered dejectedly from room to room.

The place was full of memories for her, and she felt a lump rising in her throat as she looked at the dining-room where she had served so many meals to Rob, the kitchen where she had told him her incredible pack of lies, and the swimming pool where Rob had exacted such a wet revenge. Fighting down the tears, she made her way to the telephone in the study and called the airport. Yes, they could give her a ticket on the six p.m. flight from Rainbow End to Perth. No, she wouldn't need to be at the airport until half an hour before departure. Jo hung up the phone and sighed. She should have been pleased. She was leaving Rainbow End, and she never had to set eyes on Rob Challender again, so why did she feel like crying?

At least there was time for a cup of coffee before she left, and after that there would be only one task left undone. She would have to find somebody to send out to pick up the others from Clarrie's camp. The fragrant

smell of coffee was just beginning to fill the kitchen when
she heard the sound of wheels in the driveway. Her heart
leapt involuntarily, and she ran to the window. But it
wasn't Rob. The big, red-faced man in the khaki shorts
and shirt was a complete stranger to her. But he knocked
at the back door as if he knew the place well. Jo opened
it cautiously.

'Hello,' she said warily. 'Can I help you?'

He touched his hat to her.

'G'day, missus,' he said., 'I come to the back door
because me boots are too dirty for the front. I'm Dave
Fisher, Ted's brother. I believe Ted went out towards
Cutler's Springs with the Challenders today. Is he back
yet, do you know?'

'No, I'm sorry,' replied Jo. 'They're still out at Clarrie
Brown's camp. Can I help you at all?'

Dave grinned.

'Don't reckon so, love,' he said. 'Not unless you've got
a rifle I can borrow. I'm goin' roo shootin' tonight, and
Ted generally lends me his. Anyway, now I know where
he is I'll drive out and see if I can catch up with him.
Thanks, mate.'

He turned as if to go.

'Wait!' cried Jo.

Dave turned with an enquiring look on his face.

'Could you do me a favour?' asked Jo. 'I was supposed
to drive back out to the camp and pick up Ted and the
others, but something's come up and I have to catch the
plane to Perth. Could you give them a lift back to town
for me?'

'Yeah, too right,' agreed Dave readily. 'Here, listen. I
could drop you off to the airport on me way, if you like.
How would that suit you?'

'That would be wonderful,' said Jo fervently. 'If you
can come in for a moment, I'll just get my bag. Or
would you like some coffee before we leave?'

'Why not?' drawled Dave, strolling into the kitchen.

'Mind you, I reckon we'll all be drinking somethin' a bit stronger by the end of the evenin' if what I hear is true.'

'Oh?' said Jo cautiously.

'Yeah. You must have heard by now, love, if you was out there with them. About that nugget Old Clarrie's supposed to have found. They reckon it's near as big as the Golden Eagle.'

'Golden Eagle?' asked Jo blankly.

'The largest nugget ever found in Western Australia,' explained Dave, accepting a steaming mug of coffee. 'Discovered by James Larcombe in 1931, but, if the rumours are true, this one of Clarrie's will run it close. I tell you what, love, you don't want to go flyin' off to Perth tonight if you can help it. Yer gunna miss a hell of a party here in Rainbow End by the sound of things.'

'Yes, I suppose so,' conceded Jo sharply. 'But it can't be helped. I have to go!'

Dave cast her a baffled look.

'But this is one of the finds of the century!' he protested. 'They'll paint the town red tonight celebrating. Don't you want to be there?'

Jo thought of herself whooping it up with Tom and Clarrie and Rob. Dancing dizzily with Rob, sipping champagne, rubbing shoulders with Miranda.

'No!' she said fiercely. 'I don't. Now please can we finish our coffee and go to the airport?'

Dave's heavy features set into an unhappy scowl.

'I'll take you to the airport, love,' he promised. 'And I'll go and get the rest of the mob, but I reckon you're making a big mistake.'

An hour later Jo was pacing restlessly up and down the Rainbow End airport, waiting for the plane from Perth to arrive so that she could fly out of Rob's life forever. She had hoped to be left alone to sit quietly in a corner and brood, but the worst of being in a small town was the friendliness of its inhabitants. It seemed as if every second person in the airport wanted to thank her for giving them their tetanus injections, or ask her how she and Dr Challender were liking Perth. She was just making her fourth circuit of the waiting-room, when a short, fair-haired man with a moustache stepped into her path.

'Excuse me, Nurse,' he said pleasantly. 'You won't know me, but my name is Terry Hunter. My wife Beth brought our little boy Geoffrey in to see you a couple of months ago because he was playing up so much. But it turned out he had hearing problems.'

'Oh, yes!' agreed Jo with sudden interest. 'The little boy with glue ear. How's he getting on?'

Mr Hunter's face lit up.

'Real well,' he said warmly. 'Dr Challender asked us to wait a few weeks in the hope that it would clear up by itself, because he doesn't like unnecessary operations, but it didn't. So my wife took young Geoff down to a specialist in Perth for the operation last week. He came through with flying colours and, according to Beth, his hearing's already beginning to improve. Matter of fact, they're due in on the plane in a few minutes. But I just wanted to let you know how grateful we were that you spotted the problem.'

'You're welcome,' said Jo with an engaging grin. 'Oh, but tell me something else. You wife was pregnant, wasn't she? Has she had the baby yet?'

Mr Hunter's face creased into a frown.

'No, she's still only eight months gone,' he informed her. 'I'll be glad to have her safely back home, to tell you the truth. She was telling me on the phone yesterday she's been having a lot of those false labour pains. Is that a problem, would you say?'

Jo pursed her lips thoughtfully.

'Braxton Hicks contractions,' she murmured. 'They can be awfully tiresome, and some poor souls have them for a month or more before the actual birth. It usually doesn't do them any harm, but I agree that you'll all feel much better once she's safely home.'

Mr Hunter looked relieved.

'Well, I won't hold you up, then, Nurse,' he said. 'I heard you and Dr Challender had moved to Perth, so I hope you'll be very happy there. But we'll always be real pleased to see you back in Rainbow End.'

Jo smiled politely at him, and murmured something appropriate, but inside she was in turmoil. 'You and Dr Challender', indeed! Didn't the people of Rainbow End realise that she and Rob had moved to Perth for completely separate reasons? Or was the entire town determined to bracket their names together as if they were a married couple? Well, that would soon end once Rob married Miranda, she thought savagely. Not that the thought gave her much comfort. In desperation she wandered over to the refreshment bar and bought an orange juice. My relationship with Rob Challender is over, she told herself. Over. Looking out of the window at the dark sky, she saw the approaching red and green wing-lights of a plane high overhead. With a sigh of relief she drained her glass and picked up her bag.

Just at that moment the loudspeaker crackled into life.

'Could I have your attention, please, ladies and gentlemen? If there is a doctor or nurse present in the airport, could you come to the manager's office immediately? This is an emergency. I repeat. If there is a doctor or nurse in the airport, could you come——?'

The message was still being repeated over the PA system when Jo tapped smartly on the manager's door. Patrick Jennings was a brown-haired man with curly hair and a beard. His face lit up with relief as Jo entered the room.

'Jo Webster, isn't it?' he said without preamble, rising to his feet and shaking hands with her. 'Pat Jennings. You're just the girl we need. Weren't you the midwife who helped Janet Crabtree when she had that premature baby a few months ago?'

Jo nodded.

Yes,' she said slowly. 'But the baby died, unfortunately. It was so early we couldn't do anything to save it.'

Pat Jennings winced sympathetically.

'Well, it looks as though we've got a similar case on our hands tonight,' he revealed. 'There's a passenger on the Perth plane that's due in any minute now, and apparently her membranes have just ruptured and she's gone into strong labour. They tell me she's thirty-six weeks pregnant. We've phoned an ambulance to come out from town, but if you could go aboard when the plane touches down, and help to get her safely transferred to the ambulance, I'd be very grateful.'

'Yes, of course,' agreed Jo. Then a thought struck her. 'It's not Beth Hunter, is it?' she asked.

Pat Jennings looked down at some hastily scribbled notes in front of him.

'Yes, it is,' he confirmed.

Jo spent the next five minutes hastily assembling an impromptu collection of items which might be useful. Clean towels, disinfectant, a groundsheet borrowed from somebody's camping equipment. In between organising these she tried to reassure a distraught Terry Hunter, but when the plane finally touched down on the runway she was feeling decidedly anxious herself. The ambulance still hadn't arrived, and an airport was certainly not the ideal place to try and deliver a premature infant. Fortunately Pat Jennings had everything under control so that the moment the plane came to a halt Jo and Terry were rushed up a set of stairs to the front door, while the remaining passengers were evacuated from the rear exit.

As soon as she entered the aircraft Jo heard a low, convulsive moan that broke off abruptly. The chair arms had been raised on the front row of seats, and Mrs Hunter was lying with her knees up in the confined space. A blanket had been pinned up behind her to give her some privacy, but Jo could still see a queue of passengers shuffling apologetically down the centre aisle of the plane. Swiftly she slipped into the narrow space between the seats and touched Mrs Hunter reassuringly on the shoulder.

'How are you, Beth?' she asked.

'Not too good.'

The reply came through clenched teeth, but it was accompanied by a grimace which could have been a smile.

'That's the spirit,' encouraged Jo. 'Now, will you let me just take a look at your tummy?'

But before Jo could even begin to examine her Beth Hunter suddenly caught her breath again and began to struggle up.

'I have to push!' she gasped.

'Wait!' begged Jo. 'Just pant and lie back until I see how you're going.'

A swift look convinced Jo that the birth was imminent. At the height of the contraction she could see the baby's head crowning. I wish I had a properly equipped labour ward, she thought frantically. I wish Rob were here! But she was alone, and she would have to deal with the delivery as best she could. Urgently she wrestled the groundsheet underneath Beth's arched body, and tucked a couple of clean towels into place for good measure. Then she checked the patient's pulse. As she had expected it, was very elevated.

'Oooh!' groaned Beth. 'Oooh, Nurse, can't you do something? It's so painful. I—ooh!'

At that moment there was a sudden flurry of activity in the aisle next to Jo. She half turned her head and saw Pat Jennings, the airport manager, standing anxiously beside her.

The ambulance men are here,' he said. 'Do you want her carried out on the stretcher?'

'No,' replied Jo. 'She's too far advanced. We'll have to deliver here. But get them to bring a sterile baby-bundle and a humidicrib aboard, will you?'

Jo was still crouching beside the patient, encouraging her to keep up her rhythmic breathing, when she heard another set of footsteps hurrying along the aisle from the rear of the plane. Expecting the ambulance officers, she rose to her feet and slipped out from her cramped position between the seats.

'Thank goodness you're here!' she exclaimed, wriggling free. 'She's about to deliver at any moment. Did you bring the—oh!'

For it was not an ambulance officer, but Rob Challender who confronted her. Tall, lean and overwhelming, he seemed to fill the tiny space with his presence. For a fraction of a second his blue eyes met hers with a glance that scorched her, then he went swiftly to work.

'The ambulance officers are on their way,' he assured her tersely. 'But I'll just take a quick look at her while they get their gear.'

He slipped into place between the seats, and crouched beside the expectant mother. But before he could take any action at all pure chaos seemed to break loose. The ambulance officers came in the forward door of the plane, Beth Hunter gave a final, strangled groan, and a small bluish figure shot like a rocket into Rob's waiting hands. There was a moment's silence followed by a loud, healthy shriek. Rob burst out laughing.

'Nothing wrong with his lungs, anyway, Mrs Hunter,' he quipped. 'Now we'll just get you sorted out, and you can hold the little fellow.'

Jo watched mistily as Rob delivered the placenta and cut the cord. When he handed her the tiny creature she dried it off with a towel, and then wrapped it carefully in a soft bunny-rug and space blanket from the ambulance kit. The baby mewed protestingly as the blanket tickled its face and its slate-blue eyes opened wide. Jo was smiling so hard that her cheeks ached as she placed the tiny bundle in Mrs Hunter's arms.

'Congratulations, Beth!' she said. 'He's a beautiful little boy. And not so little, either, considering he's four weeks early. A good three and a half kilos, I'd say.'

Beth Hunter gave an exhausted smile and looked down at the baby. Then her face crumpled and she began to sob.

'I'm just so. . .happy!' she choked. 'I was sure I'd lose him when this happened. I can't thank you enough. Both of you!'

Rob smiled and patted her soothingly on the shoulder.

'It's our pleasure, isn't it, Jo?' he said warmly.

Jo nodded, caught up in the euphoria of the moment. Somehow she had never felt closer to Rob than she did now, when she seemed to be floating on a gossamer cloud of joy and relief. The baby was fine, the mother was fine, everything had turned out well, and all her own problems seemed incredibly trivial and far away. She watched contentedly as Rob gave the patient an injection of Ergometrine to make the uterus contract and reduce blood loss. Then he injected a local anaesthetic into the perineum so that he could stitch a small tear. After that there was nothing much to do except for Jo to give Mrs Hunter a wash and tidying-up so that the ambulance men could take her and her baby off to hospital. Baby Hunter was put in the humidicrib for the journey, and his mother was placed on a stretcher and wrapped warmly in blankets before leaving the aircraft. Rob and Jo followed the little procession down the stairs and across the tarmac to the waiting ambulance.

'We'll call him Robert Joseph!' vowed Terry Hunter, as he shook hands with them yet again. 'Good on you both!'

Then he climbed inside, and the ambulance doors shut behind him, leaving Jo and Rob in the dark car park. As the vehicle sped away into the night Jo came down to earth with a bump. Now there was nothing else to claim her attention. Just a tall, dark-haired man staring at her with an unfathomable expression in his shadowy eyes. Behind him the lights of the runway shone like a glowing necklace in the darkness, and overhead the night sky blazed with stars. A chill wind rippled across the car park, sending leaves scampering unheeded around their feet. But Rob and Jo simply stood and stared at each other. Then at last he took a step towards her.

'Were you really going to leave me?' he asked huskily.

That warm, velvety baritone sent a quiver of longing right through Jo, but she deliberately resisted it. Remember how he treated you this morning, she told herself fiercely. Remember the things he said about you. Remember that he really loves Miranda, not you.

'Well, what do you expect?' she snapped. 'What's a gold-digger supposed to do once her cover is blown? I'll just have to go and find another sugar-daddy to exploit, won't I?'

Rob groaned.

'Cut it out, Jo!' he pleaded. 'You know I didn't mean any of that stuff I said this morning. You can't possibly believe that I really think you're a gold-digger!'

'Can't I?' retorted Jo. 'Well, what else am I supposed to think? You said it, didn't you? You accused me of setting up that farcical marriage proposal of Tom's, didn't you?'

Rob gave an exasperated sigh, and spread his hands wide.

'Yes, I damned well did!' he exclaimed. 'But it was absolute rubbish, and I knew it even while I was saying it. I know you're not like that!'

Jo's lips twisted bitterly.

'You do now!' she said angrily. 'Now that I've proved my good character by taking that stupid nugget and putting it in Tom's safe instead of disappearing into the wild blue yonder with it. But why couldn't you have just trusted me before that? Clarrie and Tom did, and they were the ones who stood to lose most if I vanished with the loot.'

Rob was staring at her with a baffled expression.

'What the hell are you talking about, Jo?' he demanded.

Jo punched one fist into the other.

'You know what I'm talking about!' she exclaimed impatiently. 'Tom's little charade this afternoon out at Clarrie's camp. Giving me the gold nugget to take it into town and put in his save in order to prove to you that I could be trusted. So you're finally satisfied now that it's in Tom's safe, are you? Well, bully for you! But I don't need anybody who wants that sort of proof before he can trust me!'

Jo's eyes filled with angry tears, and she folded her arms protectively around her body, shivering in the chill wind and stamping her feet to keep them warm. Then suddenly Rob's powerful arms were around her, and he was staring down intently into her angry face.

'I don't know what the hell you're talking about, Jo,' he insisted in bewilderment. 'This stuff about nuggets and Tom's safe is beyond me. All I know is that one minute I was talking to Miranda out at Clarrie's camp and you were sitting in the jeep, and the next minute you'd vanished. I realised then what a damned fool I'd been, so I just went after you. I shouted my lungs out, but you either didn't hear me or wouldn't stop. Anyway, I ran down the road for a mile or so, and finally managed to hitch a lift into town. I turned the place upside-down looking for you, and then I realised you'd probably be catching the plane to Perth. So I came here.'

His hands were warm and urgent through the thin material of Jo's blouse, and he gazed down at her with a passion that made her feel weak at the knees. Then she remembered her last view of him at Clarrie's camp with Miranda in his arms, and she hardened her heart.

'Well, that's very nice,' she said in clipped tones, dragging herself free of his embrace. 'But it really doesn't change anything, does it, Rob? If I ever need a character reference I'll ask you for one, but in the meantime I've got a plane to catch. So I guess this is goodbye, Dr Challender.'

She marched briskly across the car park towards the

lighted terminal building, but Rob sprinted past her and
blocked her way.

'Like hell it is!' he exclaimed.

And he dragged her into his arms and kissed her with
a fervour that made her throb with desire. For one wild,
intoxicating moment she kissed him back, putting every
ounce of her yearning and love and fury into it. Then
she struggled free and marched on. Rob grabbed her
impatiently, and swung her back to face him.

'Would you stand still while I'm asking you to marry
me?' he roared.

Jo's throat went suddenly dry.

'What did you say?' she whispered.

'You heard me!' retorted Rob. 'For God's sake! What
do you think this is all about? I've been trying to propose
to you since last night, but every time I get to the point
somebody has a bloody baby and interrupts me!'

Jo looked uncertainly down at the ground. It seemed
firm, but she could have sworn that a shock measuring
nine point four on the Richter scale had just passed
through it. She cleared her throat.

'You didn't want to marry me this morning,' she
pointed out hesitantly.

'Well, of course I didn't!' exclaimed Rob. 'Not with
Tom holding a gun to my head. I told you I wanted to
make my own matrimonial arrangements!'

Jo swallowed.

'I thought you meant Miranda,' she said in a small
voice.

Rob locked his hands around the back of her head and
drew her closer so that he could nuzzle her long, curly
hair.

'Oh, no,' he denied softly. 'That's well and truly over,
my love, and don't you ever think otherwise.'

'But you had her in your arms this afternoon!' protested Jo. 'I saw you!'

'No, you didn't!' exclaimed Rob with fervour. 'I had
my hands *on* Miranda's arms, that's true enough, but

there was certainly no love lost between us. I was telling her how selfish and hard-hearted and grasping she was for trying to cheat Clarrie out of his claim, and she was abusing me for being naïve and wet behind the ears!'

There was a moment's silence. Jo gazed searchingly into Rob's intent blue eyes.

'Truly?' she whispered huskily.

'Truly,' he assured her. 'Look, Jo, Tom may have messed things up today, but he was right about one thing. All that glisters isn't gold and, when you come down to it, Miranda is mostly glister. But you're the real thing, my darling, there's no question of that. And I love you more than I can tell you.'

This time when he gathered her into his arms and kissed her Jo made no attempt to escape, and there were two minutes of blissful silence. Then at last Rob released her and gave her a playful shake.

'Well?' he demanded. 'Are you going to marry me or not?'

Jo's lips curved into a smile. Reaching up, she threaded her fingers through his thick dark hair so that she could draw his face down to hers. Then she kissed him slowly and sensually on his warm, open mouth.

'Yes,' she said firmly. Mischief danced in her eyes. 'On one condition.'

'What's that?' demanded Rob, mystified.

'That you offer me a car and a trip to Hawaii!' she replied.

Rob's delighted chuckle rang through the car park. He caught her against him and hugged her till the breath was squeezed out of her. Then he tucked her hand firmly in his.

'Come on!' he commanded. 'I hear they're painting this town red tonight, and we don't want to miss out on the action!'

Eighteen months later Jo Challender lay exhausted but triumphant in the Dalkeith maternity clinic in Perth, with a tiny, red-faced bundle clasped lovingly in her arms. The door of her private ward opened softly, and Rob tiptoed in with a bottle of Bollinger on a silver tray with two tall glasses.

'Do you always do this when you deliver a baby?' asked Jo sleepily.

'Only when I'm in love with its mother,' responded Rob, setting down the tray on the bedside locker and lounging on the edge of the bed.

With one deft brown finger he folded back the edge of the white shawl and smiled at the tiny, crumpled face beneath. Then he picked up the bottle and eased the cork out with a soft pop. Vapour coiled in a lazy trail as the champagne bubbled energetically up. Pouring out the golden liquid, he handed a glass to Jo and then picked up his own drink.

'Well, here's to my beautiful wife Jo and our fine son Thomas Robert,' he said proudly, clinking his glass against hers.

Jo sipped the champagne and paused, smiling wistfully.

'And to the memory of the original Tom Challender,' she reminded him.

Rob smiled too, and raised his glass.

'To the original Tom,' he agreed. 'An obstinate old cuss, but a man who knew pure gold when he saw it.'

Then he set down his glass and kissed his wife very thoroughly indeed.

— MEDICAL  ROMANCE —

The books for your enjoyment this month are:

CROCK OF GOLD Angela Devine
SEIZE THE DAY Sharon Wirdnam
LEARNING TO CARE Clare Mackay
FROM SHADOW TO SUNLIGHT Jenny Ashe

♥   ♥   ♥   ♥   ♥

Treats in store!

Watch next month for the following absorbing stories:

A SPECIAL CHALLENGE Judith Ansell
HEART IN CRISIS Lynne Collins
DOCTOR TO THE RESCUE Patricia Robertson
BASE PRINCIPLES Sheila Danton

Mills & Boon

Discover the thrill of 4 Exciting Medical Romances – FREE

FREE

BOOKS FOR YOU

In the exciting world of modern medicine, the emotions of true love have an added drama. Now you can experience four of these unforgettable romantic tales of passion and heartbreak FREE – and look forward to a regular supply of Mills & Boon Medical Romances delivered direct to your door!

❧ ❧ ❧

Turn the page for details of 2 extra free gifts, and how to apply.

An Irresistible Offer from Mills & Boon

Here's an offer from Mills & Boon to become a regular reader of Medical Romances. To welcome you, we'd like you to have four books, a cuddly teddy and a special MYSTERY GIFT, all absolutely free and without obligation.

Then, every month you could look forward to receiving 4 more **brand new** Medical Romances for £1.45 each, delivered direct to your door, post and packing free. Plus our newsletter featuring author news, competitions, special offers, and lots more.

This invitation comes with no strings attached. You can cancel or suspend your subscription at any time, and still keep your free books and gifts.

Its so easy. Send no money now. Simply fill in the coupon below and post it at once to -

**Mills & Boon Reader Service, FREEPOST,
PO Box 236, Croydon, Surrey CR9 9EL**

NO STAMP REQUIRED